Brantwood

Also from Carcanet
The Man in the Iron Mask

Brantwood

THE STORY OF
AN OBSESSION

PETER
HOYLE

CARCANET

First published in Great Britain 1986 by
Carcanet Press Limited
208–212 Corn Exchange Buildings
Manchester M4 3BQ

The author wishes to thank North West Arts for
assistance under the Bursary scheme.
The publishers acknowledge financial assistance
from the Arts Council of Great Britain.

British Library Cataloguing in Publication Data
Hoyle, Peter
  Brantwood: the story of an obsession.
  I. Title
  823′.914[F]   PR6058.09/

  ISBN-0-85635-637-9

Typesetting by Pen to Print, Colne
Printed in England by SRP Ltd, Exeter

To Tom Dunne
for encouragement and practical advice in the writing of
Brantwood and *The Man in the Iron Mask*

PART 1: 1929

An Experiment in Biography

'When John Ruskin died at Brantwood on the shores of Coniston Water, 20 January 1900 "the book of Brantwood was closed forever".'
— H. D. Rawnsley, *Ruskin and the English Lakes*

'He wanted the hour of the day at which this and that had happened and the temperature and the weather and the sound, and yet more the stillness . . . the slant on the walls of the light of afternoons that had been. He wanted the unimaginable accidents, the little notes of truth for which the common lens of history, however the scowling muse might bury her nose, was not sufficiently fine. He wanted the evidence of a sort for which there had never been documents enough, or for which documents mainly, however multiplied, would never be enough.'
— Henry James, *The Sense of the Past*

ONE

Our projected study of John Ruskin's last years, a joint venture by my cousin and myself, subtitled, 'An Experiment in Biography', was based on shorthand notes of conversations with people who had known Ruskin at the end of his life. Warwick and I disagreed on many matters but we were both convinced that the attention of biographers should now be directed towards the final years, the years that had been neglected or deliberately misrepresented to protect the sentimental 'great Victorian' image and to obscure the tragic reality of his decline.

In the late summer/early autumn of 1929 we made a definite start on the project.

My own interest in Ruskin began in early adolescence. The author of *Traffic* and *Unto this Last* did not attract me at all but I knew *The Ruskin Reader* almost by heart. This was a small volume of selections by W.G. Collingwood (at one time Ruskin's secretary and the author of the first Life), taken from *Modern Painters*, *Seven Lamps of Architecture* and *The Stones of Venice*. My cousin's enthusiasm for Ruskin was of more recent origin — a surprising development actually in view of his previous wholesale disparagement of the literary achievements of the Victorian age.

In the first flush of his enthusiasm, Warwick devoured an enormous quantity of Ruskin's writings as if he could never be surfeited. Warwick is more articulate than I am and he has a very precise, retentive memory. Before long he seemed the more knowledgeable. However I was always afraid that the ardour of a convert might spend itself prematurely, like a much earlier enthusiasm for Shelley. Even when his admiration for Ruskin was at its height, Warwick could be scathing about certain aspects of the great man but, at least at the outset, he maintained that we could not have found a subject to equal Ruskin for rich variety.

— The man was so full of vital contradictions, he asserted.

— As complex as a character in Dostoevsky . . .

— Of undisputed significance historically . . .

— A writer with commanding natural gifts . . .

— A youthful intensity of vision that remained with him till late middle age . . .

Beneath a calm exterior Warwick was volatile, moody, and (usually) iconoclastic. From the first I had grave doubts about how long his positive commitment to the project would last. But my cousin had always been self-willed and ambitious. I hoped I might rely on a combination of his ambition and his father's sneers to sustain the long haul of our enterprise. (Warwick's father was a martinet schoolmaster and so reactionary that he classed Ruskin with the founding fathers of Bolshevism.)

Our original plan had been to interview as many surviving relatives, friends and acquaintances of Ruskin as we could trace. We began our interviews in London. I volunteered to take verbatim notes, in a personal kind of shorthand that I had been practising for many weeks. We considered ourselves exceptionally well-equipped to record such personal reminiscences. My cousin's phenomenal memory had served him well at school and university.

Before long we decided to revise our original plan of collating the accounts of a large number of people. Instead we concentrated on the testimonies of a dozen or so individuals, relaxing this rule in one case only to admit the testimony of a 'surrogate', the close friend of someone who had been right at the centre of life in the Ruskin household in the final decade but who steadfastly refused to speak to us.

Our first important interview was with Arthur Severn, inheritor of Ruskin's Lake District house, husband of Ruskin's cousin, the late Joan Severn. Joan Severn would have featured at the head of our list of people to see had she still been alive.

We had sent our letter of introduction to the widower's home in Warwick Square. A rheumaticky old man, not unlike Thomas Hardy in appearance, received us.

In a rather senile way perhaps, Mr Severn was intrigued by the coincidence between my cousin's name and his own London address. This coincidence seemed to predispose him in our favour.

We listened to anecdotes of a trip to Italy, Ruskin's illness at Matlock, and his disastrous last visit to the continent. As well as information that was relevant to our purposes there was a great deal that was marginally relevant and wholly irrelevant. As the afternoon progressed and my wrist started to ache, I was sure that many of the pages of hieroglyphics that I was amassing would find their way into the wastepaper basket.

Encouraged to bring away Mr Severn's unpublished reminiscences of his life with the great man, we found that these contained almost all the useful material that I had painfully wasted so many pages on and that could be much more conveniently extracted from Severn's manuscript. Mr Severn seemed doubtful whether his memoirs of the 'Professor' would ever be published. In private we agreed; or at least not until the day when every contemporary document relating to Ruskin was considered worthy of publication.

The preparation of a list of carefully drawn up questions —. my own and the questions that Warwick had in readiness — proved to have been effort totally wasted. Mr Severn was too old or too temperamentally discursive to confine himself to

5

giving specific answers to specific questions. He would make mysterious allusions in passing. More than once he referred to 'The Woman in Black'. But he appeared bewildered and suspicious if we asked him to enlarge on what he had just been telling us.

At times the old man was remarkably forthright about the Professor, but he was even more likely to be coyly secretive where there seemed no need at all for reticence. May be, over the years, he had acquired the habit of prevaricating in the face of direct questions — part of the Hush! Hush! No Scandal! tactics that had been the order of the day at the turn of the century.

It was difficult for us to appreciate what the care and secrecy had been all about; for example, just how the Rose La Touche affair could be seen to compromise Ruskin; on the surface a somewhat excessive devotion to a young girl and to her memory were the only indiscretions he could be accused of.

On our second visit we apologized for mentioning Mr Severn's late wife. If the subject was too painful we could pursue another line of inquiry. On the contrary, our host assured us he would be glad to talk about Joan.

Our first question was how demanding had Ruskin been of Joan Severn's time and energy? What effect had this had on their family life?

Mr Severn for once made a direct, predictable reply.

He said that while Joan had never ceased to be an exemplary wife and mother, her preoccupation with the Professor's problems had, from time to time, given grounds for disquiet. And the particular form the Professor's illness had taken had made it difficult for the rest of the family, with the best will in the world, to be always sympathetic.

In one or two outbursts, for which his rheumatism was perhaps partly responsible, Severn described the problems of living with an ageing, mentally unbalanced genius.★ The most memorable of these outbursts occured during our second visit. Severn told us about Ruskin's insane suspicions when he was undergoing one of his attacks of brain fever.

— To have wild accusations thrown at your head! exclaimed Mr Severn. To be told in ringing, imperious tones that you were conspiring against him with the sheep in the field below! Why, gentlemen, it was hard to hold on to your own sanity! Joan was a tower of strength. But even Joan needed a rest from time to time. Towards the end it was rather less of a problem. The Professor brooded more, was quieter. As his physical infirmities grew, you understand. Anyway, we had to make a life of it, for the children's sake. The house wasn't a morgue. And for us, living there, it wasn't a shrine either.

Severn emphasized how listless and feeble Ruskin became.

— There was no real conversation with the Professor in the last years. Visitors called to pay their respects, look at the pictures, the view of the lake. Even his oldest friends hardly got a word out of him. No response at all really. I'm speaking of the last years now. Yes. No. Yes. No. In a toneless little voice. Collie used to get on my nerves, acting as though Joan and I were somehow to blame for the Professor's sad condition . . . (There was a good deal more, in the same vein, in criticism of W.G. Collingwood, Ruskin's former secretary and first biographer, before the old man returned, with some coaxing, to the subject in hand).

We could appreciate how awkward Severn's position had been at Brantwood, financially dependent on the Master in an ambience far from congenial. Arthur Severn was the kind

---

★'Genius is not a word Arthur Severn ever used in connection with Ruskin. There was no recognition of Ruskin's outstanding gifts in any remarks we heard from the son of John Keats's friend. The single reference he made in passing to Keats and to his father was when he expressed a doubt that Keats was ever as much trouble for one half hour to Joseph Severn as Ruskin had been constantly over so many years.
NB 'A good fellow', Keats wrote of Joseph Severn, 'but his nerves are too strong to be hurt by other people's illnesses.'

of man who talked far more naturally of 'yacht and regatta' than of art. A photograph on his desk taken before the turn of the century showed a sporting gentleman, damp-eyed, with a droopy moustache, and a suggestion of smoking-room cynicism that gave him the appearance of a Galsworthy philistine, the husband in a picture by Orchardson, a regatta man of the Tissot era. A jovial manner and the authority of the marriage tie with warm and dependable Joan, must have made him tolerable to Ruskin; but we did not see Arthur Severn adapting easily to a household dominated by an idealist Master who kept early hours, who banned smoking and vetoed all forcefully-expressed contrary opinions.

— When he was on his high horse, Severn told us. I'm speaking now of earlier times. When he was writing those letters to British workmen, the Professor was best left alone. Agree with him or disagree with him, he wouldn't be satisfied. Tell him the mist on the lake was pestilential, he would say it was beautiful. If you said it was beautiful, he would say it was damnable. And yet to his lady friends, like the old ladies of Thwaite, he would pretend all his rages were nothing. Just saying naughty things. By which he meant fierce things. He would promise to change, to be all sweetness and light and milk and honey, in the future, once he had roasted . . . toasted and roasted . . . some bishop or other. Women could handle him far better than men. To be of the male gender and get on with him, you had to keep a tight rein on yourself. To have your own opinions, to defend them stoutly, oh he didn't like that at all!

— The Professor had a strong personality, Severn continued. But he was eccentric and he was not manly. Old maidish the sort of life he expected us to lead.

Of an evening the Professor read aloud. The only light relief would come if the cat walked over the page and made the candles flicker with its tail. The ladies took up their needlework. The men, the artists/secretaries and Severn, sketched as one of the Waverley novels was read to the household.

We were left wondering whether Mr Severn had failed to complete his occasionally vivid memoirs because there had been too much unpleasantness associated with Ruskin: ugly scenes as well as the humble pie he had been forced to swallow in the interests of financial security. Collingwood later confirmed that for Arthur Severn the Professor had been an embarrassment, a burden and a bore, a morbid fanciful man subject to alarming tantrums and absurd whims. Severn must have found it galling to watch his wife mothering their benefactor in a cloying unnatural relationship, as though 'Dear Coz' and not her husband and children, were her chief concern. (Even if it was, with her too, essentially a question of money.) In parts Severn's memoirs were shrewd; occasionally they were penetrating. For example, his comment that Ruskin was a poor judge of character. Ruskin's published works show little interest in psychology. People and events he saw by the light of the ideal if impressed; if horrified and disgusted he judged by absolute moral criteria, condemning from on high, never making the slightest effort to understand or identify with the point of view and material circumstances of those he condemned. And Severn's remarks about Ruskin disliking the night gave us food for thought. If it was true, as far as Ruskin was concerned, that nature ceased to exist when the sun went down, that agreed so well with what we knew of him and his dislike of 'shadows of the street and of the boudoir-curtain', of night-pieces, Rembrandt's chiaroscuro, Whistler nocturnes, falling rockets. And he shunned nocturnal passion (as much when church-blessed and officially-endorsed as when illicit or mercenary). Again, it was always the darkness in the pollution of nature that he stressed. No metaphor. For Ruskin darkness was literally satanic, the devil's black book.

9

Warwick seemed in a bad humour as we came out into a raw foggy London afternoon. I thought it was high time we made the journey to see Ruskin's Lake District house and got to grips with the unpublished material. We had the address in Coniston of W.G. Collingwood. We knew we would find Severn's youngest daughter at Brantwood. And surely there must be people who remembered Ruskin. A tradition of stories current among the Coniston locals. Arthur Severn had given us a short list of names, people who might be of use to us. (In the event we discovered that a number of them had been dead for some time, and, in the case of former family servants, it seemed astonishing that he should not have known this or should have forgotten.) Warwick's attitude to Severn was coloured by a fancied resemblance between the latter and his father. Oddly, the old man had not mentioned his daughter Violet at all. From other sources we had heard that she was shy and unapproachable. References to Collingwood had been consistently disparaging. For this reason alone Warwick considered there was a good chance that Collingwood would prove immensely useful to us.

In extenuation of Severn's prejudices and his inexplicable vagueness at times, I reminded Warwick of the man's great age. He must be nearly ninety.

— He treated us like schoolboys, Warwick said with feeling.

— Be fair to him! I said. He did reveal some quite novel facts about Ruskin. About Ruskin, the absent-minded professor walking out into the streets of Verona in his dressing-gown and slippers. And Ruskin perched on scaffolding. Always your man for heights, the Professor . . .

— Don't forget what he said about you! said Warwick. You have the Hapsburg lip. Like King Alfonso. And the little verse he spouted to us.

Death comes to church
On King Alfonso's wedding day.

10

— Most people accept that an old man is licensed to make personal remarks now and then and be a little crazy, I said. An old man's crotchets. He seemed quite taken with you.

Warwick did not regard that as in any sense a compliment or an honour.

We started to make arrangements for our trip north. Warwick and I had been to Wales and the West Country. Warwick had even been to Ireland but neither of us had been to the north and the Lake District. Warwick professed a deep-rooted abhorrence for Wordsworth and the Lake poets generally. It was part and parcel of his extreme views on many subjects. Also his father venerated Wordsworth. Warwick believed Ruskin should have settled in Switzerland rather than Coniston.

— Each time a new hotel was put up he would have had a breakdown, I used to argue.

— In that case he should have settled in Italy or Austria, Warwick would continue to argue.

Warwick had the fixed idea that the Lake District was so bleak and inhospitable that it had harmed Ruskin. When Ruskin became too ill to make his annual journeys across the continent, the rain and the cold and the darkness of the north had deepened the melancholy that settled in the wake of a series of nervous breakdowns.

I was much less certain than my cousin about the connection between climate and mental well-being. And I expected from the Lakes a more intimate, friendlier landscape than the mixture of grandeur and dreariness Warwick evidently anticipated. In the event it was the study of Ruskin's unpublished diaries, rather than his firsthand experience of the Lake District, that were to confirm Warwick in his conclusions about Ruskin and the final years.

The older he got, Warwick argued, the more essential the variety of travel became to Ruskin — weeks or months in the sun, the relaxed way of life of the Mediterranean countries

11

after the muffler-and-top coat tedium of the long northern winter.

— Only children benefit from the lessons of boredom, Warwick said. At times Ruskin needed to 'bask in dreamy benignity of sunshine'.

Warwick imagined Ruskin in age — seated by a window overlooking the black lake and menacing sky (his beard gleaming like a waterfall in the dimness) until the hour when a 'Grey Sister of Aglaia' brought in the lamp. And although he knew very well that in his extreme old age the Severns would not have allowed their charge out of doors unattended, Warwick pictured Ruskin alone, motionless, like a standing-stone, impervious to the rain, or, if in motion, roaming the moors like the old Leech-Gatherer in his own world of visionary dreariness. Warwick suggested that we might find Ruskin there still. As we tramped across the fields towards the foothills, we might catch sight of him outlined against the sky high above us, transformed into some imperious basaltiform shape perched on a crag.

It was during the last week we spent in London that we decided to restrict the number of people we would interview. This followed a couple of dismal interviews, including one with an ancient beldame who had once been a young housemaid at the Ruskin house at Denmark Hill. Her endless senile chatter like the so-called reminiscences of another old retainer gave us nothing that we could use.

Neither were we at all satisfied when we had produced a first-draft chapter devoted to Arthur Severn's reminiscences. It was difficult to construct any sort of a connected narrative out of what he had told us. And his most vivid memories had all been of a time long before the years on which we intended to concentrate. Though it was only natural that Arthur Severn should take a keener pleasure in recollections of his younger days. And sickroom memories (in this case of the years after Ruskin's health had broken down) are not the sort of memories anyone is eager to recall.

There were many gaps we were disappointed he could not fill. But even if he had been willing to make the effort, it was unlikely that he could have resurrected what had obviously made such a feeble impression at the time. Arthur Severn had travelled whenever the opportunity presented itself; he had fished and boated on the lake; he had led his own life as far as possible, painting and chain-smoking in the specially built studio at the back of Brantwood. At this time it was plain from what Severn told us that Ruskin had simply 'mouldered', becoming increasingly inactive. Like the central figure in a patchily faded fresco that has become spectral, while subordinate figures have lost none of their original distinctness, he had imposed himself less and less on his surroundings. Joan and the others, perhaps Joan Severn almost alone, since hers was the only name the widower mentioned in this connection, had had to talk *to* him and *for* him to create a specious sense of life still circulating about him. In actual fact the Master said nothing, did nothing, and only rarely in any but a disagreeable way reacted noticeably to external stimuli.

Severn's most evocative memories, memories of the late 1860s and 1870s, included Ruskin wearing a cocked hat made out of a newspaper on a scorchingly hot day at Lucca (a detail that, incidentally, with details from other sources, appeared in a dream I had on the way to Coniston); Ruskin on a paddle-steamer on Lake Geneva, the day he threw aside a yellow-backed novel with such vehemence and thoughtlessness that it went overboard to be cut to shreds in the paddle-wheels; Arthur Severn complaining to the authorities in Venice, on Ruskin's behalf, about the insufferable noise, and the nonplussed officials who genuinely could not understand what offence could be caused by the cries of hawkers or the whistle-blasts of naval boats and other steamers, the bustling pride of the New Italy,

13

and even an ironclad of the *Professore*'s own Royal Navy on a goodwill visit to *La Serenissima* . . .

Obviously it would not do to simply appropriate without due acknowledgement the most memorable passages from Severn's manuscript in which some of these incidents occurred, and so our disappointing chapter was peppered with quotation marks and included the above-mentioned incident of the complaint about the noise in Venice and also a strikingly evocative description of a storm that occured while Ruskin and a party of friends were staying at the *Danieli* when there were floods in the Piazza and Piazzetta with tables and chairs floating by . . .

Of course, if we had adhered rigidly to our declared objectives, we should have excluded these altogether. We salved our consciences by admitting them as background material to eke out Severn's vague and monotonous later memories.

I remarked to Warwick that dank and dismal though Brantwood and Coniston might have been for a good part of the year, Ruskin was not as tormented by noise as he would have been had he settled abroad. In support of Severn's evidence I mentioned the remarkable letters from Venice in *Fors*. Warwick particularly admired these. He argued, with a good deal of truth I believe, that the evocation of the steam-whistle of the *Capo d'Istria*, that had tortured Ruskin in his Venice apartment in the summer or autumn of 1876, is paradoxically intensely pleasurable for the reader — more so than many descriptions where the intention has been to share a pleasure with the reader — not because the reader likes to gloat over a vivid account of mental suffering, but because indirectly it is so complete a rendering of the sights and sounds of a particular morning in Venice; the sunlight and the rich variety and essential inviolable beauty of the setting is conveyed along with the registration of an agonized discomfort that (with the message he was struggling to

14

formulate for his audience of English Working Men) was the author's direct concern.

Whether this was true or not, such descriptions reinforced Severn's anecdote. They proved Ruskin to have been a man at least as much of a martyr to the noise of the streets (and waterways) as Carlyle or Schopenhauer.

Warwick still believed Ruskin had mouldered and had suffered unspeakably at Brantwood in those last years not only because his health had foundered but because he felt himself a prisoner. It was incredible that he could have been content to vegetate in the provinces all year round. Many times during the last decade, he must have woken with something of his old spirit and said to himself: Today I will set out for Chamonix! Today I will set out for Venice! And but for the Severns' discouragement (their own interests requiring that he remain under virtual house arrest), Warwick was convinced he would have done so.

— I thought you said once he had petrified into a fossil, I reminded him.

When we resumed conversations of this kind, it was during what became regular walks by the shores of Coniston Water. By then Warwick had to admit the whole region was far less bleak and inhospitable, far softer and more sylvan (even on the threshold of winter) than in the imaginary pictures he had painted in London, which were more appropriate perhaps to the climate and scenery of Norway or Iceland.

15

TWO

When Ruskin's first biographer, W.G. Collingwood, was engaged on the Life in the early 1890s, he must almost have considered he was writing about a dead man. We expected Severn's youngest daughter, Violet, to provide us with information about those largely uncharted final years. No matter how gauche and unsophisticated Violet Severn turned out to be, we were confident that we could overcome her shyness.

In November, therefore, we set out for Coniston, hoping to have lengthy conversations with this forbidding middle-aged unmarried daughter of Arthur Severn, who lived alone in Ruskin's lakeside house.

The train journey took us the greater part of a day. Warwick re-read *A Portrait of the Artist* in a new pocket edition. I had Cook's biography of Ruskin on the seat next to me but a good deal of the time I sat back with my eyes closed. There were tedious delays and several changes. Somewhere north of Crewe I woke from a dream about Ruskin that derived in part from Severn's reminiscences but also, I think, from the famous Tenniel illustration of Alice sharing a railway compartment with an eccentrically-dressed gentleman and a goat of human size. In my dream it was Ruskin who wore the 'paper boat' or cocked hat of the man in the white paper suit. His companions were a convict in broad arrows and a beautiful young girl who lay bound and gagged on the floor between the shins of the male travellers. Wearing the coy pelican smile of the *Punch* Whistler cartoon, Ruskin kept his head averted from the girl captive on the

16

floor and from the unfettered, brutal-faced convict opposite him. His attention seemed exclusively directed at the passing scene outside. Perched at the very edge of his seat, and with his body pressed against the side of the carriage, Ruskin's whole attitude suggested the most intense eagerness, bordering on inane rapture, an eagerness that he made no effort to conceal or restrain, often springing up to hang far out of the open window; any moment I expected that his cocked paper hat would be snatched away . . .

When I woke the train was approaching a dismal manufacturing town over a long curving viaduct. The first objects to catch my eye were a sooty municipal clock tower ringed by much larger factory chimneys belching dense smoke. Both of us were unfamiliar with the industrial midlands and the north. Warwick was fascinated by the spectacle of huge, four-square, brick spinning-mills and the countless smoke-stacks that we had only seen before on photographs and on engravings advertising merchandise. He made the comment that one of the tallest chimneys, apparently modelled on St Mark's campanile and just then not smoking, provided an ironic counter-balance to the description in *The Stones of Venice* of a smoking belfry producing a sullen cloud over the glamorous city. A much larger cloud of smoke hung over each of these dank, forbidding mill towns, with some finer scrolls and fainter paraphs of urochrome or white vapour issuing from slender steel pipes on the outskirts that bordered dull green fields.

'Scoria towns in Slagheapland' was how Warwick described Wigan and Warrington. He said he would like to take photographs of the factories, the mines, the spoil heaps, and especially the brimstone ponds and 'baleful streams'. As we passed through the bigger stations he drew my attention to the fact that it seemed almost a statutory obligation for them to display a model of an Isle of Man steamer in a glass showcase. Warwick was unimpressed by my Ruskin dream. He considered that I had such a highly-developed, artful,

17

self-conscious imagination, I stage-managed my dreams in the act of dreaming. We put away our books. Around Lancaster we admired a ghostly bay and estuary at twilight. There was a brief distant view of the Lakeland fells in the afterglow of the sunset.

It was seven o'clock before we finally reached our destination. Since leaving Carnforth it had been too dark to make out our surroundings. At Coniston the dimly-lit booking-hall was deserted but for an elderly man in a caped overcoat. Warwick threw down our tickets on the barrier by the empty ticket collector's cabin and immediately a gust of wind carried them away into the darkness behind us.

Perhaps something in our appearance or demeanour repelled or frightened the last of the Severns to remain at Brantwood. Violet Severn refused to speak to us on the subject of Ruskin. An unattractive, broad-faced woman of fifty or so, she seemed distrait, brusque to the point of rudeness, and literally waved us away from the porch.

After several fruitless attempts to arrange a further meeting, we were compelled to approach a surrogate, Mrs Caroline Rigby. Mrs Rigby (née Stalker) was a former friend and near-contemporary of Miss Severn who lived with her husband and invalid mother not far from The Sun Inn where we were staying.

We hoped this indirect approach would merely be an interim measure.

From our intermediary we learned that during Ruskin's last decade, local people understood something of the situation up at the house but to visitors they presented a united front, expressing only the pride they felt in the presence across the lake of the venerable and celebrated genius of Coniston. And the locals were invariably respectful if they chanced to meet the great man with his valet, taking his usual funereally slow walk south of Brantwood to Beck Leven and his rustic seat. Local people had a high regard for the cousin who looked after Ruskin in his later years. Mrs Severn was considered a very affable, kindhearted, and gracious lady. The only exceptions to this opinion that Mrs Rigby knew of were one or two members of the Master's St George's Guild, who were jealous of the Severns' special relationship with Ruskin. They accused Mrs Severn of selling the pictures off the walls and substituting copies painted by her husband so that the helpless old man wouldn't be violently outraged.

Mrs Rigby dismissed these as malicious, monstrous fabrications.

— I knew Violet Severn and her mother too well, she said. I am sure all the family were basically kind and considerate towards the sick Professor. You must remember though what a difficult man he was to deal with. And his age.

Violet had undoubtedly feared Ruskin, Mrs Rigby told us. It was his madness she feared, his attacks, his demented shouting at dead of night. Violet regularly lay awake listening to his terrible rages and his pitiful tearful outbursts. She had been afraid to wait on him in his study where he ate alone. The overwhelming fear she felt, even though he was old and frail, had made her speak of his death as the end of a nightmare. For her the blackness of years had all at once dispersed.

— This had not been her mother's attitude, I remarked.

— Certainly not. To her mother there was no one to equal 'Dear Coz'. A figure to be loved and venerated. To help him had been a privilege despite all the heartache and problems.

In later years Violet spoke of the shame and guilt she felt over her instinctive loathing of the old man. She came to realize how dependent the family had been on him for the way they lived, the house, the holidays, her brothers' education. And no family relationship to speak of. Her mother's baby talk to the old man had revolted the young Violet. Years afterwards the memory of it still disgusted her.

— But she could weep, said Mrs Rigby, when she thought of her mother's goodness of heart. Violet was her mother's favourite, by the way. Arthur Severn's favourite child had been Lily. He never seemed to care much for Violet . . .

Mrs Rigby was a big-boned, robust, homely-featured woman, taller and in every other way bigger than her genial, easy-going, pipe-smoking husband; she was intelligent, articulate and, fortunately for us, she liked to be precise; only once or twice did she go off completely at a tangent. Mr Rigby had a likeable, much less dominant personality, and if we tended to treat his reminiscences with rather less respect that was perhaps simply because he lacked his wife's air of authority. In disagreements over questions of fact Daniel Rigby usually deferred to his wife; he admitted her memory was more reliable.*

We asked the couple if they had heard of 'The Woman in Black'. Was she a well-known local character?

Mrs Rigby shook her head.

— Sounds like a novel, said Mr Rigby. Sorry! That was *The Man in Black.*

When we revealed it was Arthur Severn who had spoken of 'The Woman in Black', Mrs Rigby told us bluntly that if we had no more to go on than that, she didn't think we would ever discover the woman's identity. Many elderly women used to wear black all the time.

The Rigbys had two cats: a rather thin tortoiseshell cat called Snip which had disappeared soon after we arrived, and an enormous, impressive Persian called Mazzie. (After Mazawattee tea.) To the Rigbys' amazement, since they said she was very retiring as a rule, the Persian settled on Warwick's knees. I felt rather aggrieved that Warwick was able to sit back and stroke the cat while I was hunched

---

*Actually, on paper, the husband's reminiscences proved almost as useful as the wife's and I think we were unduly influenced by his less authoritative or less serious manner as he relaxed with his pipe, and underestimated his help.

forward uncomfortably over my notepad. Not until the huge cat moved to curl up by a fruit bowl on the rep tablecloth did I feel that Warwick really began to listen and concentrate.

After the cat had jumped off his knee and Mrs Rigby had apologized about Mazzie's hairs, Warwick asked her what Arthur Severn's attitude had been to Ruskin. The reply was, as we had expected, that compared to her mother, Violet's father more or less ignored the old man in his final years. Although, not long before the end, Severn had painted him; probably to please his wife.

We had seen the result. The result had been a faithful old dog by Landseer. Like Dignity in *Dignity and Impudence*. By all accounts the great man had been pathetically grateful for this canine metamorphosis.

— So much better, Mrs Rigby commented, than those photographs that made him look like an orang-utan.

— But in Violet's opinion the photographs were closer to reality, she added. His eyes, Violet used to say, were nothing like the soulful, sorrowing eyes in her father's picture. The real eyes were frightening. The gleam of madness in them.

Mrs Rigby reminded us that the valet was always at hand. Just in case. To prevent the Master doing anything silly or objectionable.

Mrs Rigby could not recall that Violet had ever described any really objectionable incident.

— He swore sometimes. I suppose that wasn't very edifying, given his reputation for high-mindedness. Violet claimed she only felt safe with him when her mother was in the same room. As far as I know he never harmed anyone. He never presented any terribly unedifying spectacle that might have caused a scandal.

We were told Ruskin used to frighten Violet by pressing his face to the window of a room in which she was sitting and smiling vacantly at her. And it pained her when he grasped some object, his hat for instance, or his repeater watch, or his stick, and with childish obstinacy refused to let go. But

21

Violet never suspected him of doing any real harm. If Mrs Severn discouraged the village girls from calling for games, instruction and cream buns that was because of the Master's extravagant fancies. There was the danger of him disinheriting the whole Severn family for some pretty little chit who reminded him of his not-to-be-spoken-of Irish sweetheart.

— Rose La Touche, you know, Mrs Rigby explained unnecessarily. She had died a long time before.

— Nevertheless he frightened Violet, I said.

Mrs Rigby nodded. But in her opinion what had frightened Violet most was the alertness of her parents and the servants to the first signs of trouble, as though everyone was waiting for a storm to break. Dangerous doors opening. Angry doors slamming. Doors hurriedly closed on his shocking rages. Whenever the doctor was sent for, the possibility had to be faced that keepers might have to be sent for too. As a girl Violet went in constant fear that the family home might become a private lunatic asylum.

Mrs Rigby stressed how Violet had despised the fussy, self-important pilgrims who venerated the great man's name. They used to wait reverently in the entrance hall, not expecting (perhaps not desiring) to be admitted. They paid their respects in galoshes and ulsters, holding wet umbrellas, nodding sympathetically, and talking as if they were in church.

In Violet's opinion they were all hypocrites, too conscious of their own worth to be genuine disciples. Their complacency and vanity disgusted Violet. Even her mother's good friend Professor Norton, the American, had made her uneasy despite his beautiful manners and air of kindliness. She had once heard him call the Master an anachronism. He may have said 'Saintly Anachronism'. Still it had sounded very patronizing and Violet had felt differently about his beautiful manners after that, and his measured Harvard tones.

22

Warwick's eyebrows went up when Mrs Rigby spoke of 'Harvard tones'. When I asked her about this, Mrs Rigby insisted she was quoting Violet's very words. Mrs Rigby had quite a fund of brief anecdotes about the Ruskin pilgrims. For example, once young Violet had overheard a clergyman refer to her mother as 'The Manageress' while his clerical companion had simpered, in imitation of Mrs Severn's apparently fulsome but genuine smile. It seemed that Violet disliked the clergymen visitors most of all because of their unctuous manners, and any slight to her mother used to rouse her to fury.

We made the obvious comment that our hostile reception by Violet must have been a result of a lingering prejudice against these 'pilgrims'.

— And Violet was happier when the old man died? we prompted Mrs Rigby.

— Much happier. At least for a time. A great sense of release. A more normal sort of life for them all. Also the stream of visitors became a trickle. You know how reserved Violet is. Thank goodness! Violet would say, the house was never opened to the public as it seemed he had wanted. It had been enough of a museum while he was alive. The old Guild Members used to say that the soul left Coniston whenever the Master was not in residence. If this were true, Coniston must have lost its soul for good when 'the book of Brantwood was closed forever'. That was Canon Rawnsley's phrase. Violet had no time for Canon Rawnsley or the old lady Guild Members.

The couple described the history of Brantwood after 'the book was closed forever'. The early years of the century had been a time of prosperity for the Severns and extensions were still being made to the house up to the Great War, Daniel Rigby thought. His wife wasn't so sure. In recent years the house had deteriorated, especially after Mrs Severn died. Typhoid carried off Violet's sister. Violet didn't get on with her father and he very largely

23

ignored her existence. He lived permanently in London after his wife's death.

We had told the Rigbys that we had been to see Arthur Severn at his house in Warwick Square. There was a noticeable coolness whenever his name was mentioned.

— I am sure he will have found some foolish woman down there to look after him, Mrs Rigby said tartly.

— Does he ever travel from London to visit the house? we asked.

— He pays short visits but only when he wants to find something else to sell, was the reply.* He probably blames Violet for the condition of the place. I don't suppose he thinks of paying for any repairs.

I asked why Violet had broken with her old friends in the village.

Mrs Rigby did not know.

— I have never myself had a real quarrel with Violet Severn, Mrs Rigby insisted. People will tell you she is happiest on her own. It may be so. I find it hard to believe. Of course she spends a lot of her time out rowing on the lake. She is her father's daughter as far as that goes . . . The house has become so uncomfortable, so draughty and leaky . . . I believe there are saucepans and pails everywhere to catch the rain . . . Have you been inside the house at all?

— Only as far as the entrance hall, I said.

Warwick murmured:

— Like the pilgrims of old. The *passionless* pilgrims.

Mr Rigby leaned forward and knocked his pipe out on the hearth.

— It can only be healthier for Violet to be out in the open, commented Mrs Rigby, frowning at her husband. She must have a strong constitution. Of course poor Violet must know she will have to leave soon. When her father dies if not before. But who will they find to take on the big dark

---

*This was, in fact, hearsay. The couple had not seen him for many years.

24

crumbling leaky place with its grounds mostly hillside? The children round here call it the haunted house.

— Why is that? I asked.

— For no reason, said Mrs Rigby, except that it's big and neglected nowadays. And remote from the village.

On our second visit, Mr Rigby surprised us by saying he had known Peter Baxter, Ruskin's valet in his later years. The valet was fond of talking about the winter months the Master had spent alone at a seaside resort on the Channel coast. Warwick asked numerous questions. Apparently Peter Baxter had struck up a friendship with the housekeeper of an elderly spinster in the town. Most of what Baxter had told his friend had been on the subject of the love affair with the housekeeper but some incidental light was shed on Ruskin.

On one occasion the valet had spent most of the day with the housekeeper. (Supposedly, in agony with toothache, he had been out in search of a dentist.) Late afternoon, as it was getting dusk, he felt something like panic at the prospect of returning and had run all the way back to the sea-front cottage the Master had rented. And yet when he arrived it was plain Ruskin was unaware how extraordinarily long his absence had been. The Master was sitting at a table by the window, a closed book in front of him. The lamps had not been lit. The flames of candles were blowing about in the dark, chilly room. Baxter lit the lamps with trembling hands. The Master seemed calm but listless and melancholy. He made one remark, a strange one, that his books were like dead things on the wall. Baxter had been afraid it would be a case of the ominous calm before the storm. At best he had expected the Master's languid spirits to persist the rest of the day but in the evening he had brightened considerably and had wanted to play chess. He even drank a little wine before going to bed rather later than his usual time.

— Perhaps I should explain, Mr Rigby told us, that the Master kept very regular hours. He went to bed very early. It

25

was the very worst time of the year to be at the seaside. They had every kind of dirty weather except snow. But the Master had been in such poor spirits he said he preferred days that were overcast.

According to Baxter, Ruskin had been writing his life story at that time. Now and then he would require help in recalling a particular incident, a forgotten place-name, a date, the name of an acquaintance. Baxter was convinced most of the incidents the Master wanted his help in recalling had happened long before his time. But his chief preoccupation lay with his earliest years and of course there were few people still alive to help him there.

— Peter used to say he was the right sort of person to get on with the Master. He was patient and tolerant. He had no 'temperament'. No imagination. He seldom lost his temper. The Master liked to shake his head over Peter's total ignorance of learning and the arts. A good-natured block-head, he used to call him. Affectionately.

The Rigbys were hazy about what year it was that Ruskin had spent the winter months on the south coast. Mr Rigby was uncertain which resort it had been. In this respect we were better informed. Daniel Rigby hazarded a guess it was some time in the 1890s.

Evidently Mrs Rigby had listened many times before to the story of Peter Baxter's romance with the house-keeper. The woman had been married (although long separated from her husband) and so there had been no real chance of anything permanent developing for them.

Ruskin had known nothing of the romance. When the time came Baxter had been very reluctant to leave the little watering place. Resentful. In general, Mr Rigby told us, Peter Baxter had been very loyal to the Master. In word and deed. He would not hear anything said against him. He was more critical of Arthur Severn although he got on well with the rest of the family. Arthur Severn often spoke disparagingly of the Master. That was one reason why Peter Baxter disliked him.

— Every morning old Mr Ruskin used to describe his dreams to Peter, Mr Rigby said.

When I asked if the valet had ever discussed Ruskin's illnesses, the reply was not in any detail. Peter Baxter had been a steady, reliable servant, not a man to tell tales about his employers. In fact he had rarely spoken about the Master. His interest in those seaside months had been on account of his own romantic attachment.

— It was very sad really, commented Mrs Rigby. It seems he still talked about the woman years later. She had told him she would look him up when the old spinster died and she got her promised legacy but I don't believe he ever heard from her at all afterwards.

I asked Mrs Rigby if she could describe to us what Violet Severn had been like as a child.

— She was very thin, the good lady began. And she had a sickly sort of complexion as a girl . . .

Mr Rigby looked as if he were about to speak. But remained silent.

Knowing that I was less concerned with Violet's appearance than her personality, Warwick said:

— I think my cousin means was Miss Severn as retiring then as she is now?

— Yes and no, said Mrs Rigby. Violet was always quiet but there was something very beguiling, teasing, about her when she was a girl. She had a lively curious mind. A lively fancy. But I suppose it is true to say she never was very talkative or sociable.

— I always thought it was a pity Violet never married, added Mr Rigby.

I made very few notes of the conversation, not wishing to lose sight of our chief objective in a wealth of detail about Violet Severn. I was still hopeful that eventually we would

27

persuade her to talk about her memories of Ruskin at Brantwood. In which case much of the information we were gathering at second-hand might well prove of limited value.

The Rigbys were goodhearted people, anxious to be helpful, but it seemed unlikely that we would profit very much from another afternoon spent in their company.

Before we left, Mrs Rigby insisted on taking us upstairs to see her bedridden mother. I was rather shocked by the poverty-stricken appearance of the old lady's room. In one corner of the ceiling a few laths were revealed where the plaster had fallen. Old Mrs Stalker gave us a toothless imbecile smile. Although only a woman in her late sixties, she seemed quite senile. She spoke in monosyllables, in a tiny little voice, and did not seem equal to the effort of having visitors at all. Warwick made no attempt to be nice to the old lady. He gazed out of the window (the room overlooked Yew Tree Road and the inn where we were staying) while I stood for a few minutes with Mrs Rigby next to the bed. We had been told that Mrs Stalker had been on intimate terms with Ruskin's cousin but it was immediately obvious that she was incapable of communicating to us her experience of the old days.

When we came downstairs again, Daniel Rigby told us that as a boy he had once seen Mr Ruskin with young Violet in the village.

His wife seemed doubtful that this could have been so.

— Are you sure, Daniel? she said. Here in the village?

Mr Rigby pondered for a few moments and admitted his mistake. It was down by the lake he had seen them. Somewhere by the lake. And Violet had overbalanced from a rock and fallen into the water. There had been quite a commotion.

— No. That wasn't Violet, protested his wife. That was a little girl staying with them at Brantwood. Violet used to talk about the incident you mean. The little girl was called

Venice. She was the daughter of an artist or a writer, a friend of the Master's.

Warwick, whose face had been a mask of boredom for most of the afternoon, looked mildly interested. Afterwards he remarked on the strange appositeness of Venice slipping beneath the waters of Lake Coniston. For my part I had been briefly intrigued by an image of young Violet and the aged Ruskin walking together, hand in hand, down the village street like Little Nell with her grandfather.

The old lady's quavery voice penetrated downstairs as we were leaving and Mrs Rigby called up to her mother that she would be with her in just a moment. She shook her head and smiled at us. We thanked the Rigbys for their kindness and their help. We expressed the hope that we would see them again before we left Coniston.

I was afraid that the boredom Warwick had shown at the Rigbys might signify that his enthusiasm for the project was already on the wane. But during the evening he seemed in good spirits for no apparent reason, unless it was that he had discovered a mistake in the index to the Travellers edition of *The Stones of Venice*, according to which 'Decency is a mark of excessive vice'.

— At least, Warwick said, that sounds an arresting paradox not the contrary truism you find elaborated in the text.

It caused me some anxiety that Warwick had once again taken to railing at the Victorians. Victorian taste generally, and the characteristic artistic productions of the *fin de siècle* in particular, aroused his anger and contempt.

He called the Nineties:

— That creepy, cobwebby, crepuscular decade.

After several drinks in an evening Warwick had a tendency to dogmatize and to swagger, to press down irascibly on the loud pedal, in stark contrast to his usual quiet, self-contained, somewhat supercilious manner. The self that came to the surface when he had been drinking was perhaps closer to Warwick's essential nature. At other times this lay concealed behind the conventional mask of the ex-public schoolboy and Oxford graduate — obviously a scholarly type, his personality marked by a certain hauteur but decidedly not the sort of man anyone would guess was at all likely to adopt extreme, even subversive positions in art and politics. (Rightwing then. Leftwing later.)

Warwick was an intense partisan of recent trends in literature, music and art. His heroes included T. S. Eliot, Joyce, Stravinsky, Picasso. So far Ruskin was the single exception to his anti-Victorian bias. To my mind Warwick placed undue emphasis on Ruskin's unlikeness to his contemporaries and the baneful influence of the age on him.

We knew each other so well that I had no fears that my cousin and I would be unable to work harmoniously together. At the same time I knew that if he suddenly tired of Ruskin and abandoned the project, he would take a devilish delight in discouraging me from continuing on my own. His most effective weapon against me since childhood had always been mockery. His manner, facial expression and tone of voice lent themselves only too readily to sarcasm and irony. There were several authors of the despised era that I had a particular fondness for but I rarely mentioned them because of the ridicule he invariably heaped on their names. Like Ruskin himself, the assize-court judge of art, Warwick had a gift for vituperation and I found it difficult to justify my natural preferences in the face of an eloquent, swingeing attack.

My own style had been corrupted by bad masters, Warwick claimed. And especially by the injurious example of the great pre-war Panjandrum of letters with the three manners: the mealy-mouthed, the crabbed, the ineffable.

— Your prose style is most inclined to the mealy-mouthed, Warwick told me.

30

— 'And it not infrequently thus happened that . . .' began Warwick in parody.

— Sorry, he added. That is an example of manner number two. The crabbed. The tortuous and pinched. The minutely segmented. The drily precise.

Warwick considered he was necessary to the success of our project if only to add vigour to the presentation. He could score through all my prim qualifiers: the 'perhapses', the 'somewhats', the 'rathers' that I had included for the benefit of my ideal reader, an elderly Cheltenham aunt.

Despite the wholesome mountain air and the quantity of gin he imbibed in an evening, Warwick was troubled by sleeplessness the first few nights. I told him it must be the unaccustomed silence after London. He replied that there was nothing silent about my snores and the hoot of owls. But he said he felt as though the multitudes we had left behind were still bustling and murmuring in his brain. The immense lighted Metropolis was somehow contained complete inside his brain.

During the night there was total darkness in our room and this in the centre of the village above a public house! What must Brantwood be like at night? Beneath the trees on the East Lake Road it must be impossible to see where you were putting your feet or even see your own feet and be able to tell whether you were walking in a straight line or veering towards a stone wall or a prickly hedge or about to fall headlong into a ditch. I once talked of making an expedition to see Brantwood by moonlight. I am not sure how seriously I meant this. Certainly Warwick did not consider the idea for a moment.

Since I was constantly on the look out for signs that Warwick's interest was flagging, it was a relief not long after the rather laborious, protracted second session with the Rigbys to receive our expected invitation to Lanehead, the home of W.G. Collingwood. I would be able to tell him, I

31

thought, that my introduction to Ruskin had been by means of his little 1894 book of selections. *

---

*In fact this was one of the things that I never got round to mentioning. Similarly Warwick had the impression that Collingwood and he had a mutual interest in Norse mythology but this, also, was a subject that was never touched on between them.

THREE

Setting off after lunch we discovered Lanehead to be about two miles from Coniston village; a mile, perhaps less, short of Brantwood.

Although Collingwood had been ill, having suffered a stroke, he welcomed us most warmly and introduced us to his daughter Barbara and her husband, a retired German engineer, Oscar Gnosspelius. We had a list of questions ready prepared for Ruskin's first biographer. Before we started, however, he insisted that the interview be postponed until we had familiarized ourselves with the MSS. at Brantwood. He knew that we had made no headway with Miss Severn. The manuscript material at present was being examined by a young American academic staying at nearby How Head Farm. A female, we were surprised to learn — a blue-stocking.

In our dealings with Collingwood we realized how essential it was for us to gain his confidence. On the surface we allowed him to dictate the terms of our researches.

From the beginning he declared his willingness to help although he considered the method we had adopted to shed new light on our subject was misguided. His manner was rather brusque and imperious. Essentially he was a kindly man we found.

— I believe I have learned a great deal more about Ruskin since I wrote the Life and I am certainly willing to help you, but your idea of interviewing people who knew him in his last years sounds a naïve and doomed sort of project to me. You both seem too intelligent to put your faith in that sort of approach. Believe me, you might just as well have asked the stones of Brantwood or Coniston Old Man what Ruskin was like as asked the likes of Arthur Severn. Arthur and young Violet were too near him for too long. None of the Severns shared his intellectual and artistic interests.

— Arthur Severn is an artist, I reminded him.

— An artist who has never done any thinking, Collingwood insisted. The man has no equipment for thinking. Nothing to think with. Before he became too old and stiff, sailing not painting was his great love.

Collingwood raised the subject of the American graduate who was staying with Mrs Cowman.

— You'll probably see Mrs Viljoen at Brantwood, he said. She's made a friend of Violet and she's studying the unpublished material with typical American thoroughness and energy. But she tells me she has to leave soon. I'll arrange for you to have access to the same material even if Violet can't bear the sight of you. You should have come to me first before you attempted to approach her. Violet doesn't like me much either but I'm a devil she's used to.

During the ensuing period of enforced idleness while we waited for the American to surrender her spoils, Warwick talked of making a trip to Paris to interview Jean Cocteau, André Breton, Paul Morand, Gertrude Stein or James Joyce, that other, wilder pedant engaged on making the English language unrecognizable for his second *magnum opus*. Or even Erik Satie? A year or two earlier my cousin had had a cat called Erik Satie. I believed the eccentric composer was dead. Neither of us was sure.

Probably the wintry conditions in the north of Lancashire rather than any spirit of biographical enquiry made Warwick's thoughts stray to Paris. Once he even suggested we might make a study of some recently deceased writer instead. I strangled this idea at birth. The rule was: first memoirs by friends, wives, sweethearts, secretaries, relatives; only afterwards the more systematic researches of the disinterested scholar. At The Sun Inn we imbibed rather freely. A local wit called us Mr Drunk and Mr Sober. Warwick was Drunk. I was Sober. Warwick says drink makes me more pompous and orotund. It was an odd state of affairs, Warwick said, when the critics are more bohemian than the writer under their scrutiny. Although Ruskin had been a critic himself — one who, in Conrad's words about Proust, pushed criticism to the point where it became creative.

Apart from the pub there was little entertainment in the village. A church hall picture-show that we saw advertised at the Ruskin museum featured Chaplin and other comedy shorts and a piece about agriculture in which a motor-car, its mudguards plastered with farmyard dirt and lime, drove slowly and interminably down a country lane over sky-reflecting puddles. The only memorable film, an erratic tour of Venice, that looked old enough to have dated from the earliest days of the cinema, interested us chiefly because of the Ruskin associations with the 'umquile Queen of the Sea'. Warwick claimed the cameraman must have been a giant long-legged spider or crane-fly, flitting rapidly and silently beneath the bridges of canals during a hailstorm. Abruptly this headlong nervous chase was replaced by less animated and disappointingly subfusc Venetian images. These included a ramshackle ghostly landing-stage between barley-sugar striped poles at which the high prows of phantom gondolas jostled; a group of tripod cameras with focusing-cloths left unattended in a dark and empty St Mark's square; and a bird's eye view of the long narrow iron waterspouts that droop from the eaves of the Sansovino Library. (The rifle barrels of random snipers, according to Warwick, aimed at the blurred grey tables and vague light-suited tourists down below in the Piazzetta.) A glimpse of the campanile which, because the quality of the film was so bad, we pretended to believe might be rare film of the original structure, was followed by the spectacle of a crowd pressing

35

towards a national lottery kiosk at the base of the tower, a crowd from which there emerged momentarily, close up and looking directly at the audience, a full-bearded gentleman in a wideawake and wearing a greatcoat and a large cravat who might have been Verdi or even Ruskin in extreme grizzled age. Eventually, after a distant spectral view of the west front of the Basilica, and much nearer mealy grey images of the bronze horses and roofs and cupolas, the desperate chase or flight over the canals of Venice recommenced, ending suddenly, with the stunned impact of a traffic accident, in a blank screen into which was flung a toolbag spilling phosphorescent chisels and crowbars; a dance of luminous bones followed; then a succession of enormous black letters; finally a blinding flash before total darkness.

Warwick embarrassed me by clapping enthusiastically.

We had no desire to climb Ruskin's beloved 'Vecchio'. We were not early risers. We could never have written *Mornings in Coniston*. Although, as Warwick remarked,

— How did restless Ruskin, the pigeon-scarer, manage to produce *St Mark's Rest*?

Owls kept us awake at night. Every morning we heard the blasting from the quarries that had gouged a hole in the side of the Old Man of Coniston. Late morning as we walked round by the Waterhead, the mist would still be on the water. Low cloud sometimes concealed the Old Man entirely; at other times the summit would be lightly sprinkled with snow or hail. If the steam launch *Gondola* was out on a practice run, we saw its pure white feathery smoke over the lake. As we watched, the boat often seemed to be growing larger, to be approaching the landing stage at Monk Coniston, but as a rule it slewed round and rapidly regained its anchorage on the west bank. On sunny mornings, we learned later from our studies, the lakeside had reminded Ruskin of walks by Lake Thun. Even at midday it was very cold, misty and silent as we passed the house called Tent

Lodge on the lakeside road that leads past Brantwood. Tent Lodge, we knew, had been for a short time Tennyson's home and at Tent Cottage the Hilliards had lived.

In our first week, during one of our walks by Coniston Water, Warwick recited Edward Lear's 'The Two Old Bachelors'. Ignoring the second epithet, he made the obvious comparison between the two of us and the rapacious pair in the poem who had made a savage onslaught on the sage in his mountain fastness.

— For is it not the avowed aim and proudest boast of the modern Stracheyite biographer, Warwick pronounced loftily, that he should undertake and accomplish the destruction of a sage? A Victorian sage for preference.

In this case, however, as the sage was already dead, it seemed we were safe from counterattack by his awful book though, on reflection, Warwick decided this threat was not altogether absent even now. Alive or dead, the sage's formidable work remained suspended above our heads.

We had heard from Collingwood how Violet Severn detested the Cook and Wedderburn library edition which she was far from proud of possessing. It was not merely the voluminosity of Ruskin's complete works that threatened to overwhelm her. She had no patience with the scholarly apparatus, the exhaustive double-columned index, the numerous footnotes, provided by the industrious editors. Not that she can have been the only Faint Heart to be perplexed by the index or to quail at the sight of that monumental collection of tomes.

According to Warwick, the prospect might unbalance the most intrepid and experienced Ruskin alpinist and sage-stalker and send him careering back whence he came.

Naturally, at this stage, neither Warwick nor I were seriously intimidated by Ruskin's works though it is true we had little conception then of how extensive the unpublished material at Brantwood might be.

From Collingwood we had heard that the most important manuscripts were likely to be auctioned in the near future. After Mrs Viljoen left we concentrated almost exclusively on the diaries that the American scholar had left in neat piles on the table of Ruskin's study. We realized that the diaries alone would occupy all the time we had allocated to the study of the unpublished MSS.

— Les Frères Zemgano, Helen Viljoen had called out the first time she saw us — from her ladder in Ruskin's study.

She was vivacious, the American with a Dutch name, older than we were, and full of impersonal energy. We waited impatiently for her to be gone. Even Warwick, who is more susceptible than I am, never spoke of her good looks and lively personality with enthusiasm.

Our leisurely walks by Coniston Water became a habit even after Mrs Viljoen had left and we had more than enough work to occupy us. The late mornings and early afternoons we would spend near the lake before we got down to our studies for the rest of the day and half the night. We could not always afford a fire in our rooms and borrowed a hurricane lamp to put in the window. This melted the frost on the small panes which otherwise darkened the room for us during the day. The lamp also took a little of the chill out of the air. Shadows of the lantern's bars reached out like arms across the walls of the high cold room.

Our first impression from the diaries was of a clinical element in Ruskin's observation of nature. He had studied dawns and sunsets as a doctor might examine a patient's urine; or as a man might study his own face in the glass while shaving and note his bloodshot eyes, the saffron coating on his tongue, the pimple at the end of his nose. Ruskin would study the sunrise to gauge what kind of physical and mental and spiritual state he was in. My cousin discovered an analogy with his attitude in an American novel he was reading, in which the chief character examines the sky 'like a stupid detective who is searching for a clue to his own exhaustion.' Being outward-looking, not introspective, Ruskin needed to reassure himself that he was still receptive, still equal to the task of evoking and interpreting God's signatures in nature. In his youth he had lived in a state of blessedness when the works of nature regularly gave him a rapturous pleasure. In his Brantwood years, we soon realized, the opposite was more often true: day by day he registered his losses; the whole of nature, polluted, darkened, conspired against him to undermine his faith in God. How could he fight any more for a world in which there was no inspiring sunrise?

We found that Ruskin tended to become oppressive if he occupied our thoughts overmuch and yet we could never concentrate on any other subject for long. Sometimes, for example, we tried to discuss the next European war; for we were sure it was inevitable. We told each other that we drank so much to forget future troubles. But always our minds would be drawn back to the looming presence of the Great Victorian.

Warwick declared:

— Some people might say that Dear Coz was insufferable.

— He was.

— He never found Clochette.

— Nor ever could have.

— Rose was flawed.

— His flawed glass idol.

— His chipped Galena.

A woman in a bell jar. Wasting to nothing. The jar, covered with dirt and dust, practically opaque. He had put her away. He had forgotten her. Ruskin had recurring dreams like that. A little girl he had put in a box then forgotten. A hermit crab he had packed away in his shell and starved.

A desirable residence, Brantwood, even in decay, but suburban. That flimsy, fussy little octagonal turret with its marvellous view. Those Italian windows. Pillars of Istrian stone? Perhaps. Those windows, totally out of keeping, stuck on to the house, from inside the dining-room caused disorientation. They turned Coniston Water into an Italian lake. Was that the reason why Ruskin had given the chief visible hilltop an Italian name?

One day Warwick took a fine photograph of the lake, the southern end, through those windows. Twenty years later it was still on sale as a postcard in Lakeland post-offices and sweet-shops. A perfect photograph despite the great speck of something on the glass that I had pointed out at the time. I remember my cousin's reply:

— You take a picture *through* a window. Imperfections on the glass are not out there where you focus. Out there everything is flawless.

— You must take a walk down to the dark end, the leafiest end, of the lake, past Beck Leven and Ruskin's rest, Collingwood had advised us.

It became our regular walk, as far south as Fir Island; never the other bank, the railway side. Ruskin only wished to live there when he was out of his senses.

On one of these walks I remarked that I would enjoy a gramophone recording of a selection of the noises that were most insupportable to me so that I could switch it off, at any time, just as I liked. My cousin felt that if Ruskin had been alive he would have been sympathetic to this idea; a recording of all the hoarse shrieks, the bestial howlings of the contadinos in his Italian treasure-cities that he could obliterate magically by lifting the needle off the disc. And not only human noises. All those nasty cicadas, ticking clocks, church bells, the agonies of shunted railway wagons, the rattling and screaming night and day of the cranes and whistles of the steamers that came to unload coal on the quay outside his tiny lodgings on the Giudecca. What other neurasthenic writer has left as anguished an account of the suffering caused by noise?

We were romancing, of course. Hadn't Ruskin attacked a primitive kind of phonograph as a ghastly attempt to make the dead speak out of barrel-organs? But he *had* written that he regarded deafness as a handicap with compensations for a man of his temperament. His letters to Miss Beever show little sympathy with the old lady's affliction but a powerful desire to be in a state as secure from chance interruption. Sight was the only one of the senses that he prized and by ordinary standards, past reason. For Ruskin 'the tone of time' would have no aural connotations. And a beautiful spectacle should be eternal. Not the orb-spider's 'architecture of an hour'. Not Venetial *hours*. But the *stones* of Venice.

Remembering those letters to Miss Beever (*Hortus Inclusus* 1887), I told Warwick they had contained references to Rose La Touche. The grey eyes and red cheeks that he wanted in his lifetime, not in heaven . . .

— 'I shall not want Pipit in heaven', Warwick interrupted. I continued:

— Because in heaven he would be too busy talking to the great philosophers of classical times. Since there are published references to her, how could the total obliteration of Rose have been achieved after his death even by an all-embracing series of bonfires and a conspiracy of silence?

We sensed the American had acquired some knowledge during her stay at Coniston that filled her with secret satisfaction. And yet we spent much more time studying the material there than she had done. The dreams contained in the diaries would have delighted a Freudian. But in certain moods we were strangely unimpressed, blasé. Warwick suggested we make a list of the various items of food and drink to which Ruskin had ascribed his bilious 'snaky' dreams. Our list of ingredients for nightmares included tea-cake, cucumber, hard-boiled eggs, plums, strawberries, pears, roast chestnuts, ices, Marsala, port, green peas, figs, roast ham, raisins, porridge, orange peel, *something abominable in the soup* . . . As we recited

41

them we realized how stale and insensitive we were becoming.

Miss Severn, shrinking Violet, still scurried away if she caught a glimpse of us. Helen Viljoen had found her quite delightful — a quaint old-world character with a delightful sense of humour and very helpful and hospitable once the ice had been broken. On the eve of her departure from Coniston, Miss Severn had given the American an extra-special grand tea we heard. But the sight of us only terrified the energetic recluse. (Energetic as far as boating was concerned. Collingwood shook his head at her late rising.) We despaired of piercing the armour of her shyness to discover what kind of a person she was and what precise form her delightful humour took.

Violet's feelings towards the house itself might have been ambivalent. Her love for the lake we knew to be unqualified. Taking advantage of this, Warwick waited for her one afternoon by the little jetty. It was very fresh — dashing ripples, a west wind. Warwick caught a chill and as it proved all for nothing. As soon as Violet realized he wanted to speak to her, she turned about; she literally ran from him, unconcerned that her flight was so obvious, abject, and insulting.

— Even the timid heroine of that Henry James story set in Venice was less timid than our Violet, Warwick remarked.

Her shyness amounted to a kind of illness we decided.

What made Violet Severn's behaviour all the more extravagant was that she had not been alone when she had bolted. The thin-faced young girl just behind her had looked understandably perplexed by the reaction of the older woman. Warwick had no idea who the girl was unless she was one of the gardener's children. As far as we knew they were the only other people living in the house.

— The girl looked quite ladylike, Warwick told me, perhaps a little shy herself, but she had a very bad complexion. Waxy looking. An outing would have done her good. She looked in wonderment at me before turning about. With the opposite of her mistress's haste I might add. Young Miss returned to the house with a pettish and disdainful air.

I reminded my cousin that the gardener's family no longer regarded themselves as servants. The girl would not look on Violet as her mistress. Violet Severn herself gave the impression of being a tolerated lodger at Brantwood and anyway she would not long remain as lodger or farouche mistress of the damp, draughty house.

Once, as we walked south from Brantwood, we talked about motor transport. I called it a curse of the age, certain to become a greater curse in the future. We considered the short-lived era of aristocratic 'aesthetic' motoring on deserted roads, evoked by Marcel Proust and by vivacious Proust's maiden-aunt-in-letters, Henry James; — chauffeur-driven tours of the French countryside, visits to the cathedrals of Amiens, Rouen, Beauvais, the spires of Chartres rising out of the Beauce. It was Warwick who spoke so disrespectfully of Henry James as the maiden-aunt of vivacious Proust. At times Warwick made no secret of the fact that he regarded me as something of an old woman myself. In his opinion, this explained my literary preferences for the least masculine of male authors. I told him it was better to be priggish than prejudiced. According to Warwick, Henry James was for dowagers. Incorrigibly mealy-mouthed. Cold.

With more passion than my cousin I poured scorn on the Futurists who pretended to believe a racing car was more beautiful than the Victory of Samothrace. Warwick was sympathetic to experimental art. On that occasion he let it pass.

Only one 'Devil's Motor', a bread-van, disturbed us near the south end of Colingwood's 'Thorstein's Mere'. Still, the slight yet sustained tension of expecting another gave me a premonition of the end of what the nineteenth century had viewed as a civilized environment; civilized for the élite, at

43

any rate, with the masses incarcerated in factories and foundries and offices far from Brantwood. The ignominous masses demanded excursion trains, steam merry-go-rounds at Keswick, the right to have tap water from Thirlmere, the right to see Hellvelyn while drunk . . . An unfair élitism to exclude them, I knew, I knew . . . Nevertheless it was an occasion for nostalgia surely, regret for the slower pace, for the freedom in those days from a sterile attentiveness to the dangers associated with motor transport.

The Severns had never owned a car. Did Ruskin in his twilight years ever become aware that the devilish railway would be succeeded by a more ubiquitous evil, not half a mile from his door on fixed tracks, but a mere few yards away and restricted by no timetable? His well-meaning god-daughter, Constance Oldham, to cheer him while he was alone and melancholy at Sandgate, wrote of a newspaper article extolling oil as the fuel of the future. Oil would eliminate the smoke of trains and industry. Oil would give us pure skies again. I could not believe that Ruskin would share her optimism. On the subject of the internal combustion engine, had he been alive, I was sure Ruskin and I would have spoken with one voice.

In the village we often noticed a lorry parked just by the small dank churchyard where Ruskin's greenstone Celtic cross stands. (A few years later the swastika hardly noticed at the time came to mind.) How it must have offended the sensibilities of Canon Rawnsley, who lived into the post-war motor age, and of Collingwood, to see how close the grave of their hero was to the obnoxious petrol fumes and busyness of the twentieth century! Westminster Abbey would have been more peaceful.

Joan and Lily Severn's grave and the graves of the Beever sisters, we had taken note of. Collingwood had told us he had a plot reserved nearby. We made polite noises about the emblematic cross he had designed. There was something rather pitiful about the cluster of graves — for here was the closest Ruskin came to having a family about him after his father and mother had died: his motherly, muffin-faced cousin and the elderly anthologist of his 'beauties' to be joined before long by his first biographer, the local historian and designer of monuments.

Some women were cleaning the church the first time we looked inside. Just outside the vestry door, a thin-faced young woman armed with a walking stick was beating the dust out of some hassocks set out on a small table. Suffocating clouds of dust rose up; hassocks awaiting a similar drubbing were piled against the church wall. I had mistaken them, from a distance, for dun-coloured bricks. We smiled at the girl. Warwick whispered that she was the girl he had seen with Violet Severn. She had fair hair, pale cheeks, a refined but hard expression: it was hard to tell her age. We expected a smile in return. Instead she ignored us and continued to thump the hassocks; dust rose in pungent clouds; it made us cough and splutter and whitened our overcoats.

A gas-lamp stood just outside the church wall quite close to the Celtic cross. Once I had a dream in which this lamp, atheistic and identified with Victor Hugo (the 'gas-lamp poet' according to Ruskin), conversed with the cross on the subject of the afterlife. The gas-lamp mocked the concept of an eternal father; the cross was fluent and vehement in defence of the truths of religion.

Warwick wondered if any of Ruskin's peripatetic young assistants had ever deliberately set out to deceive the Master over their commissions to record examples of choice architectural ornament and fading frescoes before they disappeared or were ruined by restoration. There had been the case of those sketches of Venetian mosaics lost in a fire in an Alpine railway tunnel.

— Not the Simplon. An earlier tunnel.

He groped for the name.

45

— Fréjus, I said. Mont Cenis rather. The fire was real.

— But was the portfolio of drawings real? Was it ever on the train with the luggage that was incinerated?

— And take that elderly copyist, Warwick resumed. Bunney. The man who spent his final years completing his commission to paint St Mark's. Perhaps he only sat down to his easel when he was sober.

— You don't believe that, I said.

Reluctantly Warwick agreed that the conscientious John Bunney, so cruelly mocked by Whistler, was probably above suspicion.* But what of the others? The younger men?

— Is it really likely that they were without exception sensitive pure serious pious disinterested honest, those artists? Ruskin was no judge of character. It would not have been too difficult, I imagine, to pull the wool over his eyes and perhaps spend months enjoying life with your mistress in Florence or Venice or Pisa with brief trips to Como when it became too hot. And then a sudden flurry of activity when the Master was expected. Blame theft or fire or rampant scrupulosity for the paucity of work to show him.

— Perhaps we should talk to one of them, I said.

— Even if we got one of his former assistants to admit to sharp practice, he would have been less culpable than the Severns, Warwick remarked. For the Severns, Ruskin was simply the golden goose.

My cousin liked to goad me into adopting a solemn priggish judicious tone where the Severns were concerned. He knew very well that Joan Severn had been daughter, sister, and mother to the old man. Even Arthur Severn had not simply acted out of self interest. He had his wife and children to consider. In the condition Ruskin was in at the end of his life, someone had to look after him.

Warwick said 'To be fair to the Severns' was becoming a tedious refrain with me.

---

*Whistler wanted to fasten a card to John Bunney's coat-tails that read 'I am totally blind'.

Frequently during our walks it came on to rain before we had reached the southern end of Lake Coniston, but the lakeside is so thickly-wooded that even in winter this hardly troubled us. Our attitude to these surroundings varied from day to day in a manner perhaps not unlike Ruskin's; a very beautiful, very pleasant lake certainly, just as Laurence Hilliard had painted it, but also secretive and sad. Youth and hope were somehow missing we felt. Towards the end of his life Ruskin had seen Fir Island as the Island of the Dead; at his little jetty he waited for Charon in the guise of his valet or the gardener to ferry him across. Obviously we accepted it was chiefly by association that we regarded the lake as melancholy, an old man's lake, even a mad old man's lake. All the same there *were* motifs that without prior knowledge might have suggested age. We noted the old chimneys, the ancestral bones, of ruined Coniston Hall, and Coniston Old Man with the open wound in its side. Ruskin had identified himself with the much-quarried hill, sulkier than the Old Man under sulky cloud, his lost life like the dirty sad blue above it, his thoughts as elevated above the thoughts of common mortals as the Old Man above Waterhead.

A solitary swan on Coniston Water, Warwick called the Swan of Tuonela. At times it was the land of mists. Cimmerian land. Hel's kingdom.

We found it difficult to imagine Ruskin walking along this road. Would the manservant Baxter have kept a few yards in the rear? Would he have stayed as close to his old master as the fool to King Lear in the storm? Another silver-haired anachronism. On a photograph we had seen of the Master with Baxter and a blurred-headed dog, the Master in his long overcoat and curly brimmed hat looked a very 'creatural' old man, beaten down by illness and age. The much slighter, wiry, alert, bowler-hatted servant held a dog lead.

— Lear and the Fool, my cousin remarked.

'Rock-rending Fors' might at times have recalled Lear in his rages. More often he seemed a Prospero figure. Not a hint of Falstaff in his nature. None of Caliban. 'A kind of angel gone astray', Charles Eliot Norton had written of him.

We had seen, too, a photograph of the Severns, friends and servants and the ancient Master seated on a chair on the frozen lake. Too trite the symbolism of that. Ruskin, his silence, the frozen lake. Ruskin had describe an earlier winter scene on the lake in 1879 when the lake had been frozen for weeks. In the night beautiful table-linen of fresh snow had been spread over the entire expanse. A black dog ran out on it. A mad scamper, a madder scamper still, and the dog was halfway across. Ruskin watched its progress from his turret. Exactly a year before this he had experienced his first 'great phrenzied illness'. The dog's paw-prints made great long irregular curves on the perfect whiteness. Ruskin followed in the dog's tracks to pay a call on the Beever sisters at the Thwaite.

On many photographs taken in the 1890s, Ruskin was less bearded prophet than grossly corporeal pathetic old man.★ The typical expression hard to interpret — half arrogant, half supplicating. Often there was nothing distinguished, nothing seignorial, Olympian, artistic, sagacious, about septuagenarian Ruskin before the camera. With his beard, long hair, interrogative bushy eyebrows, many were portraits of old age rather than greatness, of a maimed pathetic cossetted defeated old man, perplexity and self pity in his eyes. He personified Victorian Old Age more than he resembled the sensitive-featured artistic *Imperator*, with a youthful smile, of twenty years earlier. Outwardly an imposter, he might have been any retired general, judge, colonial administrator, in impotent old age, victim of a stroke, victim of senility, with ear-trumpet, in bath-chair, at Bognor, Buxton, Brantwood.

★The Frederick Hollyer portraits of Ruskin at Brantwood might be entitled *Senility* and *Sagacity*. *Senility* (the photograph of Ruskin with Holman Hunt) resembles a snapshot. The profile portrait *Sagacity* is carefully lit and posed, aiming (ironically in view of Ruskin's opinion of Rembrandt) for a Rembrandtesque effect.

One of the condemned. *Shades of Evening. The Grim Reaper.*
'Death coming nearer makes rest so dear bought.'
   — His only peace of mind was despair, remarked Warwick
sententiously, with an unpleasant nonchalance.

FOUR

When we were invited back to Lanehead we brought pages of questions, more than we expected to have time to put to Mr Collingwood even if we stayed all day and evening or were granted a series of interviews. His daughter had asked us not to tire him. He was less well than he appeared.

— Well, gentlemen. What is it that interests you most about Ruskin? The work or the life? Collingwood began.

— We did think the work, Warwick replied.

— All biographers are required to claim they are writing and researching to increase appreciation and knowledge of the work. But what really interests you most?

— Probably the life, I confessed. The work insofar as it throws light on the life . . . Would you agree that the concept of the great old man of letters or of anything else has more or less crumbled away since the war?

— I would agree that this is an age of politics and of social questions rather than of religious controversies and artistic debate. Ruskin's social ideas, I believe, are still relevant. The form may seem dated nowadays . . . Other people saw Ruskin as a great Victorian. *They* made him into a great Victorian.

— Which of Ruskin's works do you admire most today? I asked.

— I don't believe I have an outright favourite. In almost every decade of his maturity he produced a major work. The rant of *Fors* I didn't enjoy. The hostile gaze. 'The air of frantic misanthropy.' His vituperation made Ruskin many enemies. And rather undermined his cause . . . Its credibility . . . In his silent old age he was like some renowned glacier. In his *Fors* years he had been 'the angry Apennine, dark with rolling impendence of volcanic cloud'. That was his public role, you understand. In private he preferred to be likeable, even loveable.

— We abominate *Sesame and Lilies* — the 'Lilies' section, said my cousin.

— Do you?

— The tone of it, Warwick said.

I gave my cousin a warning look which Collingwood noticed and smiled.

— Ah, the tone! . . . And the form also I suspect. I think perhaps the youth of today dislikes being lectured. Unless the lecturer is Marie Stopes or H.G. Wells.

— Is it true, asked Warwick, that with Alexander Wedderburn you purged the text of *Praeterita* of controversial elements? Is the untypical serenity of that work partly due to your editing?

— That would be a gross exaggeration. Nevertheless it is true that in the Eighties he required much more assistance with his work than previously. You will notice that passages in the earlier *Fors* concerned with his youthful memories are equally serene.

— It is almost incredible to us that Ruskin could have written *Praeterita* at all given the circumstances in the 1880s. The attacks of 'frenzy'. The periods of depression. Also the number of other projects he had in hand at the same time.

— In retrospect it is incredible to me. Not incredible, knowing the man, that he would continue to work despite his melancholy and his repeated attacks of brain fever, but incredible that the quality of his writing remained so high. It was perhaps the most miraculous period of his life. Mentally and physically he was deteriorating so rapidly and yet his genius was amazingly preserved at its purest and strongest. Supported and encouraged apparently by nothing. The delicate yet so durable mechanism broke down finally at the

51

end of the decade. The wonder of it was that it had not broken down years earlier.

— My cousin and I, said Warwick, are very interested in Ruskin's state of mind in the 1880s. In the last decade apparently he could not write and rarely spoke, having lost all his former extraordinary tumultuous eloquence. But between the swarming brain of former times and the final emptiness, the 1880s appear as the watershed.

— A terrible period of his life! observed our host sombrely. Terrible the contrast between the man he became during an illness and at other times! And terrible the fear he had of succumbing yet again to one of his attacks! His desperate efforts to be prudent, to avoid what was perhaps unavoidable! Desperate manoeuvres! Titanic struggles! You know he was never as arrogant again as in the 'rock-rending' years of *Fors*. The effect of serenity, given his terrible fears and his masterful temperament, was a positive, hard won achievement.

— George Saintsbury has commented on the absence of quiet in Ruskin's prose. With the exception of *Praeterita*, a work in which 'controversy has no breathing place', would you agree with him?

Collingwood did agree in general that Ruskin's was not a relaxed style just as Ruskin was not an easy-going person. But from a bookcase he brought a copy of *Seven Lamps* and read to us a passage ending 'and lifted out of the populous city, grey cliffs of lonely stone, into the midst of sailing birds and silent air.' Collingwood claimed that this had a Paterian delicacy.

My cousin murmured:
— Joycean.
I don't think our host heard him.

Collingwood did not want us to imagine that he considered Ruskin and Pater to be writers of comparable stature. Ruskin's typically vigorous effects were the opposite of the rapt, hypnotic, suave aestheticism of Pater. Always in

52

Ruskin the freshness of the original observation showed through even after a high finish had been added to the prose. In Pater a physical detail was 'mental', 'emblematic', with no freshness about it at all. Beautiful rhythms were no substitute for freshness of observation, Collingwood maintained. Pater, to quote Pater, is for 'those who can bear nothing vehement or strong'.

Putting the book back, he went on to assert:

— The question of Ruskin's temperament is very relevant here. He was a restless man, a man of unquenchable curiosity. Not the sort of man to retreat into his work in search of peace.

In order to concentrate on taking notes I let my cousin do most of the talking and speak for me as well as for himself.

— Would you agree, Warwick said, that Ruskin loved nature through Turner's eyes? That when he turned to other artists, his enthusiasm for nature was on the wane?

— If you had known him, I don't think you would speak of his enthusiasm for nature waning. Or his enthusiasm for Turner waning. It seems to me you have an unduly pessimistic view of Ruskin in the 1870s and 1880s.

My cousin took out a portrait of Ruskin by Frank Meadows Sutcliffe. Our print was postcard size.

— May we show you a photograph of Ruskin taken in the 1870s? Would you say this is a good likeness?

— Yes indeed. A particularly fine photograph.

— We think you may disagree with our interpretation but to us the face on the photograph reveals qualities of self-love, self-assurance, even overweening self-assurance, sensitivity, and also *irresoluteness*. [Collingwood looked disbelieving.] And if this last term is a misreading of these features, the best I can describe it as is as some kind of weakness, perhaps of the saintly variety, in any case obvious enough to largely cancel out the appearance of purpose and mastery otherwise so very powerfully conveyed.

— I have heard similar comments on the Master's appearance. A cinematograph film might have given his expression better. His personality. An autochrome would be needed to render his eyes. The quality of his gaze was quite extraordinary. But as to weakness! No one who knew him, to my knowledge, has described him as a weak man. No one who knew him, that is, in his maturity, before his tragic decline.

— We hope you don't mind our broaching the subject so directly, Warwick began, but what do you think caused his attacks of insanity?

— The reason Ruskin himself gave convinces me. Because his writings, so he believed, had had no practical influence for good. That was undoubtedly one of the reasons.

— You say one of the reasons. Was Rose La Touche another reason?

— You'll pardon me, gentlemen, if I don't speculate too much on that. She was an important influence on his later life, certainly. No one would deny that.

— It seems to us, my cousin said, that the bonfire of the Rose/Ruskin letters by Mrs Severn and Professor Norton parallels the destruction of Turner drawings by Ruskin and Worum. What also strikes us is the increase in delicacy between the 1850s and 1900. Turner's nude figures were no doubt gross. But we find it hard to believe there was anything objectionable in the love letters of this most unworldly couple.

— Perhaps his friends were unnecessarily protective towards his memory at the end. It is difficult to convey how distressing those last years were. Rightly or wrongly his friends felt it their duty to protect Ruskin's reputation. It had been sullied before.

— He seems to have done so little to be ashamed of, Warwick said, pilloried for not doing something — if it was his virginity that was regarded as shameful.

— I find that rather uncalled for.

Warwick apologized.

— Perhaps you're right, our host conceded after a short silence. Perhaps it is a reasonable comment. There are many things in a man's life that will never be known. Personally I prefer it that way. Everyone knew that Ruskin was an unworldly man, an idealist, a man of unusual purity. For him to have had a physical relationship with a woman, he would have felt it necessary to reduce himself to the level of a brute. The facts of physical love I don't think he ever came to terms with. Conjugal relations were odious to him. It is well known how hostile he was to grossness, to ribaldry, in any form. But I don't care to discuss this. No doubt I'm a puritanical Victorian myself. I'm too old to change. Mr Havelock Ellis would have many opinions on the subject.

— Do you think overwork affected his mind? my cousin asked.

— Yes, I think I would agree with that although he denied it. Not simply overwork of course. Not simply quantity of work but his scrupulosity and his unquenchable curiosity. And the extreme mobility of his thought. He rarely had a holiday from mind except perhaps by sketching, chopping wood, or fell-walking. And not always then. Oh, he realized well enough that physical work was good for his mental health! . . . However. By the close of the 1880s I believe that he found it impossible to think of one thing without thinking of everything else. His energies became scattered, sometimes on chimeras, so that he could achieve no satisfying results in any one thing. Even the thought of other spheres of activity, other areas of knowledge, the awareness that they existed, or might exist, and therefore it was his duty to take these into cognizance, had as great a dominion over his mind, and came to have as much reality for him, as the immediate matter to hand . . . In the end, of course, the Prince of Language could no longer express himself, could no longer write a coherent sentence, or even utter one. He would answer 'A damn on toast' when asked what he would like for his tea. Who knows what thoughts hovered, inexpressible, tantalizingly, before him — before darting away like a shoal of minnows?

We referred to passages where Ruskin bewailed the quantity of troublous nothings in his mind, diabolic interference with his thoughts.

— The dreams are fascinating, Warwick remarked. But it seems odd that someone so out of sympathy with the sinister and gothic in literature should have such Edgar Allan Poe dreams.

Warwick quoted examples from notes we had made on the diaries: the dream of the old painting of a surgeon dissecting himself; of a man crawling *towards* a great fire; a watchmaker/mesmerist looking into the dreamer's mind; holes in his hand made by frost or illness; skeletons at a window that overlooked a radiant landscape; corpses built into a wall like statues.

— His hatred of railways . . . Warwick began.

— . . . was not too serious, interrupted Collingwood. He hated railways of course. A lot of people have hated railways.

— It strikes us as odd that Schopenhauer's defence of railways never occurred to Ruskin, great animal-lover that he was.

— And what did Schopenhauer have to say about railways? My son may be a philosopher. I am not.

— That the invention of railways was a great kindness to draft-horses, Warwick said.

— You're right, admitted our host. That might have given Ruskin pause.

I had to leave the room for a few minutes and since I was the one taking notes the interview was suspended. The interruption seemed to unsettle our host or perhaps he had been tiring before this. We decided to make an appointment to see him again in the near future. We wanted to name a particular day and time but Collingwood seemed unwilling to commit himself. Before leaving we had afternoon tea with the family.

The following day we received a letter from his daughter Barbara (delivered by hand). The gist of it was that Collingwood had had a bad night and she would be grateful if we could postpone our next visit for a week at least. Reading the letter we recalled that something odd had occurred as we had been leaving Lanehead. As we were waving goodbye, our host's shoulders had started to work up and down as if in silent, suppressed, incomprehensible laughter. It made a strange leavetaking. We thought of going back to make sure he was all right, but we were already a considerable distance from the house. Rather than seem tiresome or ridiculous, we continued on our way. We began to wonder now if Collingwood had been experiencing some kind of attack. To all appearance, he had been shaking with stifled laughter.

When we read through my notes we were rather disappointed. At the time the interview had seemed to be going wonderfully well on account of Collingwood's positive attitude and ready speech. At any rate we had high hopes of the next meeting.

We had got the impression as we were having afternoon tea (no longer note-taking of course) that Collingwood's interest in the Lake District was now greater than his interest in Ruskin. Not that we believed he had forgotten Ruskin. But as he had grown older he had grown more parochial in outlook. Only illness compelled Ruskin to be insular. Most likely, too, over the last decades, Collingwood enjoyed being a modest luminary himself, no longer shining with a borrowed light.

In Collingwood's handsome Lake Counties book we had noticed a Ruskin expression 'every pet place'. The book contains additional 'specialist' chapters by divers hands. There is a chapter on fishing by Arthur Severn. It would have pleased Collingwood if we had asked him to lend us a copy of *Thorstein of the Mere* or *The Bondwomen*. A book on his shelves entitled *Ravings and Ramblings about the Old Man of*

Coniston, he had assured us, had no connection with our chosen subject. We had asked him about Tennyson's stay at Tent Lodge. He had pretended to take offence that we thought he was old enough to have known the bard in the year *In Memoriam* was published. He had spoken at some length about Felix Hammel, inventor of the *Gondola*, a steamboat curiously exempt from Ruskin's prejudice against steamers.

Collingwood had displayed considerable affection for the little museum of Ruskin relics in the room behind the Institute, but at the same time he confessed to the feeling that a collection of personal belongings — sticks and shovel, measuring tape, geological hammer, Alpenstock and sketching umbrella — only heightened for him the loss of the man. He regretted now making copies of some of Ruskin's treasures, for instance the portrait of Doge Andrea Gritti. He would not like us to think that he had assisted at the stripping of Brantwood of its treasures but he had had of course no authority over the question of disposal of property there. He would have been sorry to see the house entirely pictureless and forlorn. Forlorn it was now, with a vengeance. Practically derelict. And whatever allowances were made, that was the Severns' doing. Even Joan, who had loved Ruskin dearly, had not been altogether blameless. A case of divided loyalties; and increasingly, after Dear Coz's death, her first loyalty had been to her husband and children.

As interesting, we thought, as any of his remarks in the short formal interview had been a comment Collingwood had made on the young friends and disciples of Ruskin — how well they had done for themselves: Blow, successful architect; Cockerell at Cambridge with expectations of a knighthood; Wedderburn, the Gravesend recorder; Sir Edward Tyas Cook KBE; even he himself, with his very modest talents, had made a certain name. And all of Ruskin's young men were eminently sane. It was as if Ruskin had taken madness upon himself to save his young friends from a similar fate. (A rather fanciful remark!) Their ambitions had been within defined limits and had been more selfish ambitions than the Master's.

— And unfortunately in this world of ours a purely self-interested ambition is less likely to have tragic consequences.

It was true enough what Collingwood said, that all the disciples had proved more worldly than their Master — without his restlessness and anguish, without his extreme guileless temperament.

A week passed and Collingwood was still not well enough to see us. We had to leave Coniston with no further meeting arranged. It was unfortunate that our last glimpse of him should have been so odd and equivocal, that is, his silent convulsive 'laughter'. On the day we left the grey smoky mining village, with its layers of terraced houses on the flanks of the Old Man, the sky above us was in 'a diabolical rage'. 'Unclean damnable railroad whistling ' summoned us to the station. In the booking hall one placard read 'Tibet Mystery', another read 'Scandal of Innocent Man convicted'. This last item we could find nowhere in the newspapers. From the carriage window we glimpsed the lake. My cousin suggested the placard referred to the treatment of Ruskin by the Almighty. Why had his young admirers deserved so much more fortunate later years? Only the self-effacing James Reddie Anderson and poor Laurence Hilliard had been exceptions among the old guard who had become minor public figures. Poor Laurence had died like a Romantic poet in his youth, in the Aegean.

The preface to our book that we wrote (in provisional form) after our study of the MSS. at Brantwood represents the high-watermark of our joint interest in Ruskin. Next summer we did not return to Coniston as planned. By then our project to interview people who had known the great man clearly interested Warwick far less.

In the preface, based largely on our study of the diaries, we wrote that in Ruskin's philosophy there was no place for the adventitious — temporarily, subjective, 'illusory' elements — in the appreciation of a landscape, a city, or work of art; Ruskin refused to accept that his own changed outlook could account for a different response. Since he judged it impossible to tire of the sublime or to exhaust a particular aesthetic seam, an outward change must have taken place. Gradually he became disenchanted with all he held most dear: an Orpheus who little by little lost his Eurydice. 'Every year', he wrote 'leaves me more lost to myself and to my memories. A gleaner in reaped or ravaged fields'. We argued that his social concern arose out of his disenchantment as well as out of his tender heart, and yet, because art and nature had less and less real power to stir him, he often felt undermined . . . paralysed . . . in his resolution to help mankind. How could he fight for a world in which there was no inspiring sunrise?

About his relations with the female sex, we wrote that to his wife he had been cold, selfish, and priggish. The word 'perfervid' might have been coined to describe his youthful prose, but clearly the man had no very ardent disposition in respect of his wife. He would have postponed consummation indefinitely with the handsome, mettlesome, worldly Effie. And twenty years later he was in no hurry to return from Venice to Rose La Touche, even though friends urged him that circumstances just then were favourable to his courtship. His ideal was located in a particular stage — April, Maytime — of a girl's development, the age of Adèle Domecq when, as a solemn youth, he first responded to feminine charms. Remaining childlike in body, a feature of her illness, the ethereal Rose preserved her appeal for him longest. Then, suddenly, on the threshold of old age, he desperately wanted the sexual satisfaction he had formerly renounced.

Of all the diary entries that we copied out and began to classify, my cousin and I agreed that one of the most central, although apparently perhaps not very significant, was the entry for 8 April 1873: 'Dreamed last night that I was in love

60

with a girl who wanted to marry me, but had at moments a bad expression of mouth, and I would not. Then a long walk in country where I was losing myself . . .' I found particularly revealing the dream of the haunted castle with one bright apartment in it that looked on to a radiant landscape, yet in the room two skeletons were standing, one right in front of the window and so impossible to ignore in any contemplation of the beautiful scene outside. A dream I made a special note of, although Warwick could not remember it from his own reading, was of Ruskin looking down from the old campanile in Venice and failing to discern Rose La Touche ('in spite of my exceptional eyesight') where she said she would be, amongst the groups and solitary idlers in the great hopscotch playground of St Mark's square. Despite his own exhortation to 'paint in black if we would be virtuous', Ruskin disliked the prominence of black — black and vermilion, black and white — in certain late sea pictures of Turner; his dream of a great naval engagement with a black steamer running away expressed not only his dislike of blackness in general, and in particular its prominence in works such as *The Burial of Wilkie*, but also his desire to see technological progress, modernism, in retreat. My cousin valued highly the simplicity and pathos of the brief diary entry: 'At Sandgate alone. Sun on the sea.' He had quoted it to Collingwood who very politely declined to share his enthusiasm for such an artless fragment. The older man regarded it as affectation to prize so highly casual effects uncharacteristic of their author. In private my cousin had called the sentences an Imagist poem, expressing Ruskin's appalled detachment from the nature he had once felt such communion with, comparable to Mr Eliot's lines '*On Margate sands/I can connect/Nothing with nothing*'. Collingwood's last words to us had been a warning against taking our 'oral' approach too seriously. He feared we might quickly tire of our researches.

PART 2: 1931

The Sale at Brantwood

'Spirits, always nigh
Though screened and hid, shall walk the daylight here.'
– D.G. Rossetti, 'The Choice'

FIVE

Collingwood's words seemed premonitory when I returned to Coniston alone in the summer of 1931. My cousin had recently embraced much more solid opportunities elsewhere and left the completion of our project to me. (Completion or abandonment. He did in fact urge me to abandon it.) Travelling through South and Central Lancashire, whenever I looked up from my reading to the anarchy outside the carriage window, I saw ugly fields contaminated by encroaching industry, cuboidal brick factories, 'family' groups of factory chimneys, old industrial scars, council housing estates, back-to-back slum terraces, polluted rivers and canals, ugliness without end under a dirty sky. The last serious discussions my cousin and I had had on the subject of our biography had been theoretical, on the ethics of the genre, the desirability, the possibility even, of biographies. My cousin had admitted the existence of rare biographies which give the reader the sense that *the* person (or *some* person) is undoubtedly there. From the majority of biographies, despite the evidence of mole-like industry, the subject is altogether absent. My cousin had become convinced ours was doomed to belong to the latter category. Then he had said we were ghouls. All critics, all biographers, were ghouls, he maintained, impotent, low-minded phantoms, although in a sense it hardly mattered because such work wasn't serious. No sane man would confuse even the best biography with a man's life.

— And not only ghouls, we are voyeurs, he asserted rather bathetically.

65

I countered this by saying there was nothing abnormal in that. Had he forgotten that, for the subject of our researches, hypermetropia had been the greatest good? Besides, the entire population would be active voyeurs if they were not so afraid of their neighbours' disapproval and dog-in-a-manger police interference.

Then Warwick had asserted we were voyeurs denied a direct view. The object of our voyeurism was inaccessible to the most industrious, the most inveterate, the most furtive and obsessed spy. The fact was that no vantage point existed to give us the view we sought and that, anyway, the freshness of our investigating impulse had been lost. The result of our endeavours would add nothing to the orthodox approach, based on letters and first-hand experience, of a Collingwood or a Cook. My cousin told me I was hanging on to an enthusiasm that had died. The ideal had grown cold. Really it was bypassable, forgettable for us now. No longer a living force in our lives. Merely conventional, sentimental veneration. We should cut our losses. Sometimes it was healthy to repudiate the past.

Warwick's worst defects I have told him often enough are contrariness and a negative supersubtlety indulged in far too freely, blurring distinctions as readily as he exaggerates differences, an engine of pure theorizing that he will not switch off. That evening I told him this once again. Instead of defending himself or attacking my position directly, he shrugged. Much later, apropos of nothing, he said that he believed my interest in the past was not primarily for people or a person but a pining for the great grey areas of emptiness that I imagined the past was composed of, an ideal beautiful emptiness that I confused with Intimations of Immortality. Intimations perhaps — experienced by the Hoary and Decrepit — for an ideal decrepitude.

— 'At Sandgate alone', he warned. 'A damn on toast.'

During the previous year, our meetings with Sydney Cockerell at Cambridge and Detmar Blow in London had not yielded encouraging results and I attributed my cousin's evident disenchantment to this. I regarded it at first as a passing phase. They were depressed times we were living in. Ruskin's star was obscured. Our own talents and credentials were altogether slighted. But in ten years or twenty a complete reversal was not only possible but likely.

It was a pity we couldn't have spoken to Sydney Cockerell and Detmar Blow (a name out of Henry James, Warwick remarked) at an age when they were more vulnerable, diffident and open, not public men with a public persona that excluded genuine spontaneity. Their reminiscences were practiced and predictable, superficially entertaining. Cockerell, whether smiling and gnome-like at home, stroking his cat, or spry, brisk and professional behind his desk in the Museum, reminded us of the chief librarian of the public library in our home town, a martinet who whistled to his staff as if they were dogs. After two interviews with him, the thought that Alexander Wedderburn might be cast in the same mould was profoundly discouraging and the fact that Sir Edward Cook was dead no longer seemed quite the irreparable loss it had done.

Detmar Blow was the more sympathetic personality. The 'annus mirabilis' for Detmar Blow had been 1888 and the day in June when Ruskin and Arthur Severn had entered the breakfast room of the *Tête de Boeuf* in Abbeville. In pre-motoring days Cockerell and Blow were staying there to visit the cathedrals of northern France, with the *Bible of Amiens* as their guide. It was a classic Victorian encounter, lesser Stanleys meet a literary Livingstone, followed by a Victorian story-book sequel, a tour of cathedrals with the great man as their guide, and for Detmar the bonus of an extended journey to Switzerland and Italy which turned out to be a darker sequel as Ruskin's mental state deteriorated. The treatment of this episode in Cook's biography is superficial and rose-coloured. In Italy the Master had been far from well. With Francesca Alexander and her mother at Bassano, Ruskin was unable to make adequate responses to their hospitality and friendly concern. He left abruptly after receiving a letter from England. At Venice, 'a grief to him', nothing roused his interest; he said he had forgotten all he had ever known about the city and was clouding Detmar's pleasure by his depression. At Merligen Ruskin was definitely ill, and in Paris his condition gave such cause for alarm that Joan Severn had to be summoned to help get the Master home. Although the trip of 1888 contained a few happy moments it rapidly became a nightmare, and marked the final collapse of a way of life that had been established with those continental carriage tours the young Ruskin had taken with his mother and father fifty years earlier.

The Master's state of mind had fluctuated alarmingly, according to Mr Blow. He had wanted to show the young man what was best of Alpine scenery and Italian treasure-cities, a sentimental journey in which no doubt he hoped to revive his own lost freshness of response in the company of a pliant sensitive student, but he was dismayed rather than appreciative so frequently, sometimes homesick for his motherly cousin and the seclusion of his Lakeland home, sometimes feverishly excited writing to a young girl in London; and, increasingly, he was confused and in a state of dismal lassitude, unable to make up his mind whether to stay longer or make a start for the north. (He even talked of going home, but not to Brantwood.) And he was pathetically grateful for any unexpected token of friendliness shown to him by the degenerate bestial inhabitants of the treasure-cities he had so often castigated 'in cathedra pestilentiae' — for example by the action of the *bonne* in Milan who helped him on with his overcoat.

Mr Blow confessed he found it hard to resurrect the self he had been in 1888. He had been over-awed, much more so than Sydney. Sydney always had a knack for establishing rapport with the great men he had sought out. And the young Detmar had become frightened by the old man's condition, by the weight of responsibility involved.

— You know, he said to us, as soon as I was in Ruskin's presence my normal self disappeared — click — and my Ruskin slave-self appeared. Even when he collided with me as if on purpose I would apologize which seemed both to amuse and infuriate him.

At Fluelen, at Merligen, Ruskin was decidedly peculiar. In Paris he was deranged. The weather was bad. Blow did not remember seeing the new giant tower. He recalled huge walls plastered with advertisements, crashing rain, intense darkness in the mornings. The immediate view from the public rooms in their hotel was over the Tuilleries gardens to the river, with the leonine Gare d'Orsay crouched on the opposite bank, but Blow spent more time looking down from a corridor window into a dismal central courtyard with ventilators, drainpipes, dirty cache-pots, and shutters, while the rain pattered on to a speckled, furrowed glass roof.

As they sat whispering outside the Master's door, Ruskin's manservant, Baxter, told Blow of previous occasions when the Master had been completely insane. More than once in the past he had begged Mrs Severn to send her husband with keepers but the situation was very difficult, very delicate. There were always envious people ready to accuse the Severns of scheming to have the Master committed so that they could gain absolute control of his money and property before he got taken by some new whim and quashed his deed of gift to them and theirs.

Detmar Blow had had one treasure to show us, the fragment of a letter picked up from the floor in their Venice hotel that he had been too embarrassed to return to Ruskin. We were permitted to scan it. Detmar would not have expected my cousin to have a photographic memory. The sentence read: 'Released from my vow, a lifetime of celibacy, the Doge and the Council of Ten have granted their

69

permission for me fully to express my love for you even within the precincts of St Mark's, my dearest Kathleen.' The draft tailed off 'Olander Pomander Gooseander'.

Sydney Cockerell had seen the Master on more frequent occasions than his friend. But not for so long at a time and he had not been as exposed to the distressing spectacle of the Master's illness. By his own admission, Cockerell, when not arranging exhibits at the Fitzwilliam, had specialized in befriending great men. Ruskin had the distinction of being the first of his trophies. The young Sydney Cockerell had made a thorough effort to make Ruskin's acquaintance and win his approbation by letter. The first visit to Brantwood in Easter 1887 had been a success. He quickly became a favourite. He received an invitation to return in the summer holidays with his sister. This was disappointed by another of Ruskin's attacks, but he stayed in the neighbourhood none the less and cultivated the friendship of Joan Severn and Sara Anderson. The following winter, again with his sister, Cockerell had responded to an invitation from Ruskin to visit him at Sandgate where the famous author had gone as though into a kind of voluntary exile, to 'stand mute, and watch the waves', perhaps doing penance for all the trouble he had caused Joan. (Ruskin stayed at Sandgate alone for months: the Rock-Limpet of the Kent coast.)

But all these experiences of Cockerell's proved to be merely preparations for the encounter with the fountain-head at the *Tête de Boeuf* at Abbeville. Apparently Cockerell did not fit into the category of servile disciple that Arthur Severn had spoken of. It is true he had held the great man's umbrella and the box of sacred (Rose) relics, but he had also risked and incurred the great man's wrath by quitting the hotel which he claimed was bug-infested. And for this transgression, after the initial explosion, he had been rewarded instead of punished, by abject capitulation to his point of view. Acceding to the young man's superior judgement, Ruskin and Arthur Severn had departed the scene of infestation.

There had been a few unpleasant incidents, Cockerell admitted. Ruskin had been insanely angry with a photographer at Beauvais. On the other hand he had savoured, with a youthful sense of fun and adventure, the authorities' suspicion over the interest the little band of art-lovers was taking in the ramparts. And of course he had enjoyed showing his young men round his churches. Cockerell commented on the rather indecent haste with which Arthur Severn had seized the opportunity to unload his responsibility for the Master on to the shoulders of the young friends. Arthur, the yachtsman, who invariably took precedence over Arthur the artist or art-lover, was eager to take up an invitation to join an aristocratic yachting party in northern waters. The attitude of Joan to this desertion can be easily imagined.

Cockerell had been envious of Blow's opportunity to travel more extensively with the Master. But as events proved, he had been spared considerable distress. Cockerell had returned to Beauvais many times after 1888. Shortly before the Master's death, he had told him this. Ruskin had responded pathetically:

— And I have not been there once, in a quavery sad sing-song voice, the voice of a childish feeble old man.

We were well aware that all Cockerell had told us had been told to others. Probably there was much that he kept to himself to use if he ever wrote about his celebrated friends. My cousin was particularly interested in how Ruskin had seemed at Sandgate. But on this subject, Cockerell's apparently successful attempt to heal the breach between Ruskin and Octavia Hill was the only information we elicited. We thought how much more perceptive we would have been than this 'lion' hunter. But perhaps also we secretly envied his success in winning the confidence of the great. Warwick could scarcely suppress his disappointment that we had learned no more of those months than how diplomatic and clever Cockerell had been. To my cousin, especially, the

71

spectacle of Ruskin alone at Sandgate, less than two years away from the ultimate collapse of his intellectual and creative faculties, pensive, confused, and melancholy, the prospect before him growing darker and darker, yet still capable of producing chapters of the serene *Praeterita*, was the most moving episode of his life.

Considering the heights to which Warwick's enthusiasm for our project was capable of soaring when time and mood were favourable, it was all the more disappointing that he could not sustain his interest or withstand other pressures and other temptations that diverted him from his course between the time we spent together in Coniston at the end of 1929 and my return there alone in the summer of 1931.

Warwick claimed we were the gravesend recorders. (Alexander Wedderburn, who had collaborated with Cook on the library edition of Ruskin's works, had been the judge at the quarter-sessions, the Recorder, in the Borough of Gravesend.) Did I not find our preoccupation with the end of a life profoundly depressing? Was it seemly, was it healthy, for two young men like us to fix our attention so exclusively on senile dementia, straining to make contact with the mind behind the silent anguish, straining to hear the echo of a death rattle across the years? Notes of sick room and death chamber. Noctuaries of the shaded lamp. Graven tablets of the Death-Sibyl.

Illogically, he also criticized our squeamishness. If we had been as thorough-going, as strongminded and clinical as the Goncourt brothers, we would have kept a vigil at the bedsides of the dying in Black Penal Homes for Indigent Forgotten Old Men to help us acquire a deeper insight into our subject. But no, although we were morbid, we were too English and idealistic to stomach that. Even 'the little notes of truth' were not sufficiently fine for us. We disdained to take notes of specific vulgarities, the great man's sloping shoulders, the dandruff fallen from his hair and beard on to his Inverness cape, the noisy expulsion of wind, the bubbles he blew with his own saliva when he thought he was alone, hours spent wearily pleating his lower lip x times per minute . . . No, what we looked for were much less palpable signs and we mistook the flap of a curtain, the moonshine on the wall, for the presence of spirits.

Warwick consistently played down the other reasons, extraneous to our research, that were undermining his dedication to the project. Really I should have anticipated that the first genuine opportunity to gain material advancement, no matter how unrelated and ultimately harmful to his literary interests, would tip the balance and he would recall nothing of our Ruskin researches except the drawbacks attending any protracted scholarly enterprise — the inevitable longueurs, the inevitable disappointments, the imperceptiveness of publishers and magazine editors, and the lukewarm support of one or two university Fellows who had seemed even excessively enthusiastic about our scheme at the outset, but later became increasingly dubious about both the likelihood of our bringing the work to a successful conclusion and the intrinsic value of our objectives.

SIX

Within half an hour of arriving at Coniston I had found lodgings. My landlady, Mrs Elms, proved a great trial. She was deaf and at the same time she was a never-ending talker, combative and malicious, a monologuist, like a dripping tap. In my room I heard the cruel sibilance that penetrated everywhere. If she was home, she was talking to friends and neighbours. If there was silence, I knew she must be out.

My rooms there consisted of a bedroom on the second floor and a narrow partitioned 'workroom' next to the vestibule on the ground floor. The latter had a handsome fireplace, too large for the room, painted pale green. On the walls there were purple oleographs of sunsets over mountains and lakes. These recalled the illustrations in some of Ruskin's books: Victorian, dated, sentimental-religiose. To my mind such pictures compromised Ruskin's own meretricious religiose nature descriptions in which he writes, for example, of the 'mighty missal pages of sunset after sunset' and of scarlet and purple clouds 'like the curtains of God's tabernacle'. It was a cold purgatory of an ugly little room in which I never did any satisfying work. The narrow room had a green-painted French window that opened incongruously on to a narrow flagged yard. The only furniture apart from an easy chair, a stand chair and folding table was a small sideboard with glass shelves at one end. As well as books by Joseph Hocking and *The Lamplighter*, the shelves contained *Sesame and Lilies* — a cheap edition with a skyblue cover, smudged as though with the landlady's trademark or stigmata of coal dust on forehead or cheek. An unpleasant

74

portrait of Ruskin faced the title pages, a Pastoral Preacher Ruskin with large hat, cataracting moustaches and beard, dressed in a hideous grey suit of Laxey woollens. On the endpapers pictures of Brantwood in 1880 from the water-colour of Alexander Macdonald. A poem had been copied out very neatly in a tiny hand on the fly-leaf. 'Thy temple face is chiselled from within' was the last line.

Mrs Elms regularly had a coal smut on her forehead or cheek. She was gaunt and energetic with a ghastly complexion beneath her weekday turban. When she was particularly displeased with me (this was all too often because I 'muttered' when I spoke at all and I left for her to scrape off my plate a turret of pie-crust and the hardest and blackest of my mashed potatoes) she looked above me towards the cornice. She was remarkable for her low cunning and self-assurance. To the least hint of criticism she reacted with the venom of a puff adder. On one notable occasion of excruciating embarrassment I came upon her unawares just as she had returned from church. Out of her Sunday hat she was drawing an enormously long pin by its great gaudy cabochon; the rapt seriousness with which she unsheathed the weapon so appalled me I turned on my heels.

Without my cousin for moral support I felt a different person in Coniston. Coniston seemed a different place. I hardly had the presence of mind to venture over the threshold of The Sun Inn. I smuggled a bottle of spirits into my lodgings. This I secreted in my suitcase and drank behind locked doors at night. I became so demoralized by unpleasant experiences with the terrible widow that I spent entire evenings in my bedrooms as though in hiding — concealed in the darkest corner from the gaze of phantoms, from God, and from my landlady.

'At Sandgate alone' was how I felt. The bleak little Ruskin museum, the churchyard, the Waterhead end of the lake, Brantwood itself, there was such an atmosphere of dread about everything that I became convinced I was sickening for influenza or typhoid. Either that or in danger of a mental breakdown. The first week, when I felt worst, I forced myself to go for long walks. Perhaps honest fatigue might overcome the morbid atmosphere in which I was submerged. From the ferny hillside above Brantwood I looked down upon the lake, transformed to copper in the light of an angry lurid sunset. It was just as Ruskin had described. 'The lake one glare of new penny.' When I saw a cloud motionless on the Old Man this brought to mind his watercolour entitled *Fixed Cloud on the Old Man*.

It surprised me that alcohol did not reduce my nervousness and disperse the morbid atmosphere. Sometimes I felt better if the day was fine and bright. One morning I woke to an extraordinary silence and then gradually I fancied that very far away I could hear a shrill tumult that might have been seagulls screeching from the Lune estuary, which surely was impossible, or if not gulls, perhaps it was children in some distant playground, a noise that was sustained and very sharp and high but practically out of earshot. As everything did that week, the remote noise frightened me, and, as I never solved what it was to my satisfaction, I came to regard it as an unearthly noise, an unearthly summons or warning.

In February, eighteen months after our conversation with him, Arthur Severn had died. At the end of the month the sale of the last effects of Brantwood was to take place. I wanted to be there to buy manuscripts and letters if there were any at a price I could afford. I persuaded myself that Collingwood would be too much of an invalid to see me. I passed Lanehead regularly but never approached his door or sat down to write a letter to him or his daughter. I wrote of my morbid state of mind to my cousin, who had become engaged to a wealthy landowner's daughter in Gloucester.

— All girls from Gloucester, he had said, are Boadiceas with sallow skins and raven hair.

In his reply, Warwick told me that what he called my neurasthenia was the hatred for all manifestations of energy felt by a person of lost confidence and low vitality. In such a mental state the world seems all swagger, all brash cliché, one loathsome hostile everlasting grimace. He said I should not confuse mere torpor, feebleness of spirit, with Pater's 'hieratic grace and precision'. Pater's recommendations and favourite qualities anyway were not applicable to real life. (In my reply I reminded him that his favourite Stephen Dedalus had also striven to 'build a breakwater of order and elegance against the sordid tide of life without him'. I must have temporarily forgotten that the result had been 'a crumbled mole'.)

'You are depressed because you have gone from one backwater to an even greater backwater,' Warwick had also suggested.

I felt an ache, an emptiness, a deep, deep, sense of loss. Loss of what?

Recently I had pinned a picture to the wall beside my bed, in the hope of improving the appearance of the room. The room if anything seemed dingier and more depressing by this addition. The reproduction was a De Chirico with a cannon, huge artichokes, moon-faced clock, symmetrical arcades, tiny puffing train, mysterious shadows. In spite of his rather doctrinaire championing of modern art, Warwick had a weakness for old-fashioned, atmospheric genre pictures, including cosy German and Dutch Christmassy snowscenes. No one in real life complained of snow more than Warwick! In his room at college I recalled there had been a snowscene of a French boulevard, circa 1880, in centre foreground, the rear view of a nubile young woman in black, elegantly dressed, tightly corsetted, with a bustle, a beribboned black hat, a glimpse of chestnut hair. Warwick said he liked paintings of women's backs. By which he probably meant their posteriors. He did have a fondness, I knew very well, this enemy of the Nineties, for Beardsley-like tall young women with broad backs and powerful haunches and with contrasting spiritual swan necks and elfin small heads — like the art student Lydia whom he had finally abandoned for this Gloucestershire Boadicea.

Warwick also liked paintings charged with an ominous silence and so naturally he approved of my De Chirico (and also of course the tentative steps he considered me to be taking towards an appreciation of the art of the twentieth century). Unfortunately, in my bedroom 'lighted like a coalcellar' I could not make the picture out clearly a few feet away, from my bed.

In recent months, out of perversity, Warwick had praised several of his former hero's *bêtes noires*; Whistler's *Nocturne in Black and Gold: The Falling Rocket*; Doré's *Spare Bed at the Crocodile* with its giant spiders and serpent; a huge naked-backed, Dutch-buttocked Venus, referred to by Warwick as 'Too much plum-pudding for supper leading to evil dreams'; also the portrait of a woman in a green dress that my cousin pretended to identify with 'the vile chromolithotint of a fat Palma Vecchio woman' waving farewell with her handkerchief from a balcony, described by Ruskin at the house of a Guild member.

The last time we had talked, Warwick had praised the Futurists, the Dadaists, the Cubists. He had even claimed to admire a certain collage of cigarette wrappers, tram-tickets, newspapers, string, chicken wire, and other 'scraps and mammocks' from the rubbish heap of modern art. He had commended to me the pronouncement of a German artist, more extreme than flinging a pot of paint in the public's face, that 'everything the artist spits is art'. In a characteristic pose, sitting forward in his chair, a cigarette in his hand, Warwick had smiled, and, wrinkling his nose supercilliously, had suggested I drop the idea of a biography and make a new selection from Ruskin outrageously different from Miss Beever's or Collingwood's, with photomontages of Venice, showing St Mark's campanile, for example, in the act of falling; Ruskin balancing in place of St Theodore on his crocodile; Rose La Touche at a café table naked except for a pot of flowers strategically placed; a Giorgione fresco like an immense cheese half eaten away by maggots; and the white horizontal waterspouts of the Ducal palace transformed into swans, which Ruskin is teaching how to fly to music and drop explosives down the many funnels of a huge paddle-steamer . . .

It was true what my cousin had written, that I saw no one at present but examples of 'human serpentry' like my landlady, who poisoned my health and mind with what Warwick called 'slavery pie' and 'the meat of the death spirit'; references — literal in part — to my account of the meals served up to me. I saw no one but harpies, furies rather, and thought of no one but a dead man. As I re-read Warwick's extravagant, long letter I could hear the landlady's shrill, venomously articulated syllables. She was talking with her equally gaunt cadaverous friends in the warm twilight of her first floor sitting-room. After a day spent at Hawkshead, I had crept upstairs past her usually open sitting-room door. But Mrs Elms's companions with their more acute hearing must have heard me; their shrill voices ceased abruptly while I ascended the last short flight to my door.

That afternoon, on the small motorbus returning from Hawkshead, I had been embarrassed on behalf of a fine-featured, perhaps consumptive-looking young girl opposite me. I imagined she must resent her elderly travelling companions, who gabbled and clocked and hooted, 'breath-ing the richest compound of products of their own digestion' — to quote my obsession, the dead man. I recognized her, after a time, as Violet Severn's young friend, the slim girl Warwick and I had seen thrashing dusty hassocks out in the open by the church porch. I recalled the contrast between the composure of her features that day and the violence with which she brought down the walking stick. On the bus she avoided my gaze. When she got down she approached a squalid cottage that I regularly passed. It had a dirty doorstep and windows and bulging, keel-shaped, incredibly soot-blackened stones. Some kind of shiny paper served instead of curtains at the upper window. On previous occasions I had noticed a black dog gazing out at the street over a potted fern from the parlour. But for the dog and the fern I might have assumed the house was derelict.

Warwick had written extravagantly and unjustly that there was a danger that my dislike of change carried to extremes might give my portrait of the Sage of Brantwood a most uncharacteristic monumental eternal arid Egyptian fixity, a total absence of light and shade. He bluntly told me he thought my devotion to the past bordered on the pathological, that documents and witnesses would never provide the insight I dreamed of. Also that my subsidiary interest in the nuance (a paradox as outrageous as Chesterton talking of 'the ancient silence of the railway station') was constantly at war with my taste for the unchangeable, my desire to arrest time and to anatomize the person and *mise-en-scène* before it develops, grows, lives. LIVES was written in bold capitals that careered so wildly down the page they proclaimed even more obviously than the letter's content the writer's inebriate state.

'I think of you in your dank backwater,' Warwick had written, 'engaged in your essentially spiritual exercises while I look over the way at purple-and-yellow tiled newspaper offices like Turkish baths. ("A terrible picturesqueness, mixed with ghastly, with ludicrous, with base concomitants.") All the windows are open on to the street and above the hawkers' cries and the din of traffic I hear the roar of the presses. Ottmar Merganthaler hath me in thrall. From time to time I read the sky for clues to your dementia — you who are the "gravesend recorder" as much as Wedderburn was.'

I deeply regretted that I had once confided to Warwick an irrational private fear that I felt my life was in danger because the tramlines I had recently stepped over now bore the weight of a metal monster, pressing down on something far more palpable than the backward-extended shadow of my

80

body. Warwick recalled this and did not hesitate to pro-
nounce it the *reductio ad absurdum* of my philosophical
position: my strange inability to accept the process of change.
Incidentally he had read somewhere that M. Bergson regarded fears of that kind — trifling, momentary, irrational
fears — as the commonplace stuff of dreams, ingredients of
the typical nightmare. If Warwick had only known from his
own experience how pertinacious such fears could be —
asleep and awake! My dreams in recent weeks had been so
frequent and lugubriously overpowering, the hoofprints of
the Nightmare should have been visible on the sheets every
morning; and during my conscious hours also, obsessional
debilitating fears and forebodings were almost always in
attendance.

As I put away my cousin's high-spirited, jejeune, but
abrasive letter (by the way he had also spoken of buying a
car), I recollected that I had seen the young girl on the
Hawkshead bus only the other day, in the company of an old
man outside the provisions store, where the sullen shop-
woman or the aggressive shopman habitually greeted me
with silence and hostile mercenary cunning. (Perhaps 'in the
company of' was erroneous and it was merely that they were
walking on the same stretch of pavement, accidentally
juxtaposed when I noticed them, the girl and the old man in
an ulster.)

A grave face, a sallow veined slender neck with the
tendons very noticeable. The features of Violet Severn's
young friend displayed 'the refinement of the dead' exhibited
by Beatrice d'Este. Thin, childlike in body, although perhaps
nineteen or twenty years of age, how far from my cousin's
Boadicea ideal of female desirability such a demure sickly
waif was! Had Ruskin's last love, Kathleen Olander, been the
same? Had she been another Rose La Touche? Or had she
been more womanly to produce in the great man such a long-
delayed perturbation and tumescence, such a desperate
unexpected longing that his body cried out for union with

81

her, the lifetime prohibition against carnal relations lifted at last? (A passion so overmastering he failed to appreciate how terrifying and unseemly the expression of an old man's lust would be to a young girl.)

It was odd that my cousin and I had never seriously considered contacting the woman who had provoked desire at last in the unworldly idealist. I made a note of it. Was she alive still? She would be elderly. I made a rapid calculation. Then I sat down seriously to write. I began: '*It was crucial to Ruskin's procedure in* Fors Clavigera *that his invective should not obscure the spectacle of his noble bleeding heart . . .*' I could write no more that evening.

It was still early but I didn't seriously consider the possibility of an evening stroll since that would involve passing the landlady's door. Instead I marked certain passages in *Fors*, including the one where Ruskin observes from the train window on the coast near Grange-over-Sands 'the sea gulls, and their quiet dropping into the pools, their wings kept open for an instant till their breasts felt the water well; then closing their petals of white light like suddenly shut water flowers.' I made a pencil note in the margin that the passage perhaps found an echo in Proust's *Sodome et Gomorrhe* where Marcel, in conversation with the literary Mme de Cambremer née Legrandin (very high flown always in her speech), finds himself talking in the Legrandin manner to please her of gulls 'motionless and white like water lilies'. Soon I closed the volume and undressed for bed. It was still daylight, the outline of the window-frame still showed plainly through the curtains, but I had already been asleep if only briefly when I imagined the landlady had shouted my name. I waited, my heart thumping, for a knock on the bedroom door. Finally I accepted it must have been in my sleep I had heard someone call my name.

On the following day the Furies had gathered early in Mrs Elms's inner sanctum. They were hissing loudly on the subject that brightened their lives — the prowler and peeping

Tom. If the prowler hadn't been elderly and as hairy as Mr Hyde in the film, Mrs Elms would have cast an eye in my direction. She viewed with deep suspicion my activities and reasons for staying in the village. The latest news was of a female accomplice who helped to furnish the prowler with young girls, baiting a trap for them, bringing them within the man's reach by engaging them in conversation in lonely spots, in woodland and down by the lake, at nightfall; at times the voices turned to excited whispers; predictably there were loud snorts of laughter too. In the local newspaper I found no mention of this prowler, but I had heard scraps of conversation at the grocer's on the same subject. One morning I was shaving at the back window and saw a farm-girl disappear into a hedge behind the houses to reappear walking across a large field full of weeds, cow-pats, and thistles. A flaw in the glass made a hunchback of the girl as she came into view, following a path that generations of feet had trodden to a whitewashed farm. A man coming into view behind her, swollen by the same flaw into a grotesque and menacing shape, became more clearly visible as a man in an old-fashioned caped greatcoat and a large hat whom I associated for a brief instant with the prowler. But the young girl, walking much faster, had reached the stile close to farm outbuildings long before the man was even halfway across the field, and I thought no more about it. Since then I had heard the prowler described as a heavy man with a stick, a shock of dirty grey hair cascading from beneath his hat, but with the bearing of a gentleman. I had heard him described also as having the look of a poacher, a tinker or Romany, very dark, with a pulpy, swollen face, wearing a heavy long coat and carrying a cudgel. A blotched face, speckled and pale, was how the grocer's wife described him to a local woman in their shop — whether from her own observation or hearsay, who can tell?

The hissing of the Furies drove me out of my 'workroom' before ten o'clock. I snubbed Mrs Rigby. I had seen her a few doors away talking to a friend. I crossed the road to avoid her. Soon I found myself in the churchyard and then within the walls of the church itself, wishing that the stark cold empty clanging nave had been less austere and darker with, here and there perhaps, a welcoming kindly blaze of candles. Instead, high above the pews, unlit electric lights hung from grey, dirt-encrusted chains, their dusty tulip shades branching out from the iron rims of giant-sized severe spiky crowns. When I sat down for a moment, I sneezed, probably on account of the dust — the hassocks by my feet were white with dust I noticed. To have snubbed good-natured Mrs Rigby filled me with guilt and added to my depression. Mrs Rigby must have hardened herself to similar intentional snubs from her childhood friend Violet Severn — if Violet ever came into the village at all nowadays. I thought back to Mrs Rigby's really rather touching account of the child Violet had been, baffled and dismayed by the presence of that mute venerable frightening figure occupying a corner of their lives, constraining and dominating her earliest years. Perhaps alone of the Severn children she had questioned the inevitability of his being there. One day, according to Mrs Rigby, she had run down to the field by the lake, shouting and crying, 'It is not his house! It is not his house!' — shouting and crying and clenching her small fists, ashamed too, aware how her outburst would have shocked and deeply wounded her poor mother. Even when Violet was a young woman and the old man had been dead some years, there were times, Mrs Rigby had told us, when Violet crept up the stairs at Brantwood, forgetting that he was no longer in his old room, or she came in with azaleas from the garden, expecting to see him at his summer desk. It occured to me that Violet might cheerfully endure a leaky roof and cracked stained buckling wallpaper because these signs of dilapidation meant the past was gone for ever; the house too sparsely furnished, too close to ruinous, too unprotected from the unblighted out-doors to harbour ghosts of the past. Formerly, so I had been told, the house was crowded with objects, rubbish according to Violet's father who had gradually disposed of the saleable items for ready cash; in the Master's day the walls could hardly be seen for pictures, and scarcely classifiable objects (amulets, reminders, relics) as well as books, minerals, shells, sketches, were deposited especially thickly in the corners where the old man spent mute listless days, uneasy unpredictable nights.

That afternoon, on the hillside behind Brantwood, I wandered for hours, meeting no one. Once I turned back at a farm gate guarded by two dogs. The dog on the left I saw from a distance; I was approaching warily from the right when a second dog emerged from its kennel, an empty cask lying on its side, close to the drystone wall; this dog was pulled up by its chain in mid-leap just short of me; it sprawled in the ruts and cow-pats in a half-strangled, thwarted fury. Meanwhile its previously silent companion, without advancing a step, the coils of its rusty chain in tussocky grass, lifted a long snout and bayed. Both animals had matted, wavy, dirty coats and bloodshot shiny eyes. Turning right about, I followed a serpentine path through bracken that was dry in spite of recent rain and the drizzle that was falling again. The wearisome frightening noise of the chained dogs, the frantic and the doleful, grew fainter. Brantwood came into view below me as I descended by zigzag paths bordered by ferns and brushwood. An hour later, from the lakeside road, the house shrouded in mist and rain showed little of the 'half-Italian air . . . like a villa set among the chestnut woods of the Apennines' described by Mr Benson. The roses in the garden had putrefied.

I knew it was madness, having undertaken this second journey to Coniston, to be making no effort whatever to resume contact with the survivors who had known Ruskin in his last years. Instead, with no intermediaries to help me, mediumistically-inspired but the medium the place not a person, I made a great effort to summon up the Master's life day by day, the image of a Patriarch with his family gathered round him — not a real family — but to all appearances a Patriarch, although the generative function had been altogether forsworn. Surprisingly, the former mother's boy and milksop and impotent husband seemed to have made a convincing Patriarch, yet before he was well-versed in this new congenial role, madness revealed how hollow the performance was — the folly of believing that a lifetime's spiritual artistic questing, carried out in perfect contempt of the grosser appetites, could end in the status of Patriarch. Then, in his last years, his reputation protected by seclusion, he became in appearance a bloated coarse old man, the sort of man it would have horrified him (in his younger, ultra-sensitive, scornful days) to be in close proximity with. Hatched and scratched by some diabolical, omnipotent Etcher to a final dark deformity — 'his face clouded with sullen thought as of a person helplessly in difficulty, and not able to give up thinking how to avoid the unavoidable'.

SEVEN

At a corner newsagents and tobacconists an elderly customer mentioned in my hearing that he believed the prowler was the image of 'old mester Ruskin' when he was alive. Except in response to prompting by Warwick and myself the winter before last, that was the first instance I recall of the great man's name being spoken in the village. The shopkeeper was unmoved. Perhaps the prowler was becoming a threadbare subject.

One night I had a dream in which, as half Ruskin, half myself, I looked down on garden, grounds, and lake from the turret bedroom at Brantwood. Everywhere, like Shelley's gad-fly, I saw 'all that sin does'. In the sky, even, creatures like flying lampreys and also devils in the guise of Seraphim mated on the wing while human lovers of a skeletal thinness, but with skins 'as white as the palmetto's beau-pots when new', lay intertwined in the garden among the azaleas and the roses that had putrefied into brown sponges. Corrupted myself by a love-philtre made from vervain, I pursued a young girl to a settlement of slate-quarrymen's huts grouped in a semicircle about the mouth of a cave. In this desolate barren place the young temptress, *Triste-Heureuse*, was exercising her pony. Erect and motionless in the saddle, like a figure in a tapestry, she wore a long mantle and held aloft St Ursula's redcross gonfalon. Before waking I had another dream. In a telegraph office a sad-faced young man made several attempts to write a message but his hand shook uncontrollably; nothing he wrote was legible, no word was completed. As if to mimic the trembling that caused his repeated failures, the room itself started to shake, windows to shatter, lamps and other fixtures to be dislodged from ceiling and walls . . .

The malaise I suffered from in Coniston was not homesickness, was not simply loneliness and the effects of a new environment, and yet I behaved in some ways exactly as I had done when I was homesick during my first weeks at Oxford, the year before Warwick joined me there. Then, I had been so abjectly miserable that sometimes, between lectures, I used to wander down to the station to consult train times and buy a stale sandwich or bun and a cup of tea as a kind of make-believe prelude to an imaginary journey home . . .

Similarly, in Coniston, during the first weeks of my second stay I would find myself drawn to the station. I would hang about the booking-hall (usually in an evening) and walk out on to the deserted platform where the wooden valances of the canopy cast vague pointed shadows. On a doorpost there was a weathered, discoloured railway map of the Lake District from which, here and there, pieces like the pieces of a jigsaw were missing, or were hanging loose, for example the whole of the top right hand corner was curled over, and in places, tiny fragile corkscrews of white paper hung down. A porter, who probably assumed I had come to the station to use the urinals, once tried to start a conversation. Once a blackbird sang very piercingly from the chimney of a small brick shed. Waddling pigeons approached if I briefly sat down on a bench. Trains were infrequent at that time of day. I do not recollect seeing any travellers or any trains arriving or departing.

During my first weeks in Coniston there had been lupins and red-hot pokers in some gardens and in the fields hedgerows of whitethorn beneath a black sky. Mrs Elms had a laburnum tree in her front garden. In early July a grey-gold dust (the pendulous yellow racemes prematurely scattered by winds and heavy showers) deadened my footsteps as I approached the shabby porch, closing my eyes as I passed through a spiralling cloud of midges.

For most of this second stay in Coniston, the weather was cool, dark and damp, with only one notable exception when the view from the Waterhead was a scene of 'strange, gilded and embalmed repose' — the lake an immense, benign, blandishing, green and golden mirror. At the spot where I was standing, among trees at the very end of the lake, there were no people, no sounds except muted birdsong; silently a glistening arrowhead widened on the surface of the lake in the wake of a solitary teal; in the remote, duskier gold reaches, far distant, a wraith of white sail, with its inverted wraith-double, was poised mid-lake as though straining to free itself from some strong bond of enchantment and begin moving in the direction of one or other shore. Eventually the golden peace was broken; the serene cloudless sky produced a monoplane with floats that hummed drowsily as it passed overhead towards Windermere.

Apart from that 'day of golden blandishment' (as I described it in a letter to Warwick), exceptions to the general monochrome were fleeting. Sometimes, after an overcast day, the sun would come out for half an hour or less, revealing streaks on windows, dust on mirrors; shadows would appear, fade, reappear, fade again.

One evening, after a fine but sunless day, I was sitting on the bed attempting to write, using the smallest of my suitcases to rest the paper on. Out of the corner of my eye I became aware of the nodding of a ragged tree shadow on a newly bright wall; when I looked round I saw also the motionless shadow of the window-frame; in a recess appeared the upright of a cross, a section of a shortened cross-piece was bent upwards across the side wall, another section, greatly elongated, was extended almost level across the sunlit back wall, then it twisted downwards like a broken limb on the narrow chimney-breast before disappearing into the empty grate that had never seen Zebra polish. The total effect was that of a twisted, misshapen cross: a fylfot to old Collingwood, designer of new Dark Age monuments, a swastika for the National Socialists whom Warwick admired.

When I stood up, the magnified shadow of my face appeared above the shadows on the back wall: huge spectacles, a nose like a woodpecker's beak attached to joke spectacles. I have never seen the silhouette of my profile without despairing. I was relieved when it swiftly faded along with the crippled, beggarly cross and the ragged tree shadows.

When all the shadows as suddenly reappeared, I turned my back on them and went over to the window. I looked through the dusty upper panes at the sky: the sun was at the edge of the only patch of blue; the clouds that covered most of the sky resembled a vast dried-up lake-bed networked with cracks; against this background a smoke-like cloud (the Devil assuming the most familiar of his many forms) was spreading rapidly in the shape of a black monster with horns, goat-head and tail.

After looking directly into the brightness I dropped my gaze to the street. A fat old woman in black appeared to be standing down below; it was the after-effect of gazing at the sun but it led me to speculate vaguely if 'The Woman in Black' that Severn had spoken of might not have been the habitual way Severn had of referring to Ruskin's ravings in his mental illnesses, his particular bugbear. What could be more appropriate, bearing in mind his dislike of darkness in nature and blackness in paintings, that such a figure should haunt his nightmares? Although, surely, if this were true there should have been corroborative references in the diaries; all I could remember from his published works was an indication of horror at a dark figure that he could not bear to look at in a painting described in art notes of some Italian gallery or possibly a church . . .

Oddly enough as soon as the phantom black shape had faded another black shape appeared — indisputably real this time. A gleaming black limousine glided by in the direction of Yew Tree Road. It was followed by a boy cyclist in a striped jersey, grinning like a monkey, riding with no hands, arms folded, close behind the car as though bringing up the rear of a procession or a funeral cortège.

Earlier in the evening I had been trying to write in the 'workroom' downstairs while Mrs Elms had been holding court in the living-room next door. I could hear every word of a conversation that ranged from reminiscences about the day when she was a young girl and had been able to sit on her long hair to how essential it was to have strong fingernails if you shopped at Wright's Greengrocers, since you had to scratch the skin off his potatoes to find out if they were blighted or not. Interest in the prowler seemed to be temporarily in abeyance.

Mrs Elms was much older than Mrs Rigby and if she had been anyone else I would have asked her if she remembered anything about Ruskin from the old days. She knew that he was the subject of my studies although no flicker of interest had shown in her face when I had told her and she had never spoken of him to me afterwards. I assumed she didn't regard him as a subject of great consequence. However, if she had possessed information she could have given me, it would have been like her to delight in withholding it to spite me.

A paroxysm of rage had suddenly seized me when, for the umpteenth time, the landlady had failed to hear what one of her friends was asking her, the note of interrogation pitched each time louder and higher. I felt my features grimace involuntarily and I gripped the wooden arms of the easy chair.

After this I had capitulated. I had picked up all the books and papers I had been using and had gone up to the bedroom. I was not out of earshot. Raised voices, sudden hysterical shrieks of disbelief and loud laughter came up the stairs, but

91

at least I was not compelled to listen to the substance of what they were saying. Later, when the landlady put records on the gramophone, the others joined in with 'O Sole Mio', 'Hear my Song . . . Violetta', and the Barcarolle from the *Tales of Hoffmann*. They were slightly less rowdy than on a previous evening, when they had been jigging and galloping like midnight hags on Walpurgis Night or the recent summer solstice, but the cracked voices of these provincial divas (like the ruined voices Ruskin heard in Venice, barcarolling for a swansig an hour) were if anything even more disconcerting and destructive to mental concentration. Mercifully the divas left soon after this. All I could hear, as the twilight deepened, was the sound of the landlady sweeping the debris of privet leaves, laburnum dust and rose petals by her front gate. I looked down on her from my window; she was resting the weight of her meagre frame on the long brush and looking along the street; above her turbanned head a cloud of midges slowly turned. I remained watching her a moment too long; she darted a glance over her shoulder up at my window; perhaps she saw the loathing on my face.

Browsing in a volume of *Modern Painters*, I came across a passage where Ruskin writes that 'the imagination is eminently a *weariable* faculty . . . incapable of bearing fatigue', which seemed to contradict what Warwick and I had written about Ruskin's inflexible point of view — one could never tire of the sublime, etc. It was, arguably, not quite the same thing perhaps but I was in the sort of mood when any statement or thought that you formulate to yourself and its exact opposite seem equally close to or remote from the truth, and truth seems lost forever in a maze of uncertainties. Perhaps in the whole corpus of Ruskin's work there was as much evidence of psychological perceptiveness and awareness of man's frailty and dependence on mood as there was of apparent intransigence and blindness to individual differences and adventitious circumstances. The same man had also written of those works of art which 'it is a duty to enjoy and a disgrace to forget', and he had uttered many other brisk imperatives that did not suggest the kind of mind that is easily impressed by theories of relativism.

When it was almost completely dark I drew the curtains and got my bottle of whisky and a rather smeary tumbler out of the large suitcase under the bed. After two doubles my senses were heightened and my powers of expression vastly improved. But next morning I discovered that what I had written before falling asleep had been no more than jottings outlining the vulgar, melodramatic theory (Warwick's originally and already a stale one, a *jeu d'esprit* that had grown whiskers) that the change to the physically almost unrecognizable Ruskin of the last years (Hyde from former Jekyll) was not the inevitable result of age and illness; that the overweight Rembrandtish, hirsute figure (the opposite of a gentleman) was really an ancient imposter, a pretender substituted by the Severns after the real son of John James and Margaret had threatened to disinherit them in favour of a pretty little chit of a schoolgirl. *'Idea for a story'* I had written below this.

I tore to shreds and screwed up into a large ball all the paper I had wasted my time blackening the night before. And I put away the half-empty whisky bottle in the suitcase and locked it.

When the landlady irrupted into the living-room with my breakfast of bacon and eggs and burnt sausage, she told me I would have to have my evening meal at six o'clock. I made no sign of having heard her as I searched with narrowed eyes on the distant wall-calendar for the dates of the sale at Brantwood. The landlady stalked off upstairs. Until she had gone out of the room, I could not manage to swallow a morsel or even steady my hand to lift a cup of tea to my mouth.

As soon as she had slammed the door shut behind her I turned my plate round so that a scallop of congealed fat near the edge was away from me. Except for a blackened sausage

93

which I wrapped in a paper napkin and hid in my pocket, I had managed to eat everything on my plate before she reappeared. When the landlady came downstairs she was holding my empty tumbler almost at arm's length. It was the first time I had forgotten to put it away. I was sure she must have smelled the whisky but she made no comment as she passed through into the kitchen. When I returned to my bedroom in the late afternoon, the clean tumbler occupied a place of honour on a crocheted doily on the dressing-table.

One afternoon, quite by chance, at the Waterhead end of Coniston Water, I met Violet Severn. I hadn't recognized her until we came face to face. Miss Severn, whose face seemed far smaller than I remembered it, returned my gaze with greater composure than I felt capable of myself.

I was determined not to frighten her away by mentioning Ruskin but there were so few other points of contact between us it was difficult to know what to say. I expressed my deepest sympathy, of course, over her recent loss; otherwise I considered it wise to steer clear of the subject of Arthur Severn. I avoided mention of the forthcoming sale at the house because that would lead to the subject of her father or of Ruskin. All the time I felt so remote from my own voice, it might have been someone else talking or a recording.

— Is your brother here with you? Miss Severn inquired.

— My cousin, I corrected her.

I told her about Warwick's new career and his fiancée. She seemed surprised to hear about the engagement. It may be she regarded us as little more than schoolboys and Warwick far too young to be thinking of marriage. I brought up the subject of university life. This gave her the opportunity to talk a little about her brothers who had been to Oxford. None of the topics we broached ever seemed likely to develop into a real conversation.

— The weather has been very disappointing, I commented.

And I quoted Warwick on Coniston in gloomy, rainy weather. He had compared it to Utgard, the domain of demons, an infernal wasteland, Hel's kingdom of mists . . .

— It was winter, of course, when my cousin was here, I explained.

Violet seemed almost alarmed at the turn the conversation had taken. I said that Warwick was apt to make fanciful remarks. Flights of fancy. I knew very little about the Norse myths myself.

— No doubt a very interesting subject, said Violet.

— The little I know sounds extremely interesting, I agreed. The giant ash-tree, Yggdrasil, binding together heaven and earth and hell. The Norns. Odin, the one-eyed old man with his slouch-hat, his mantle, his stave. His intelligence-gathering birds, Hugin and Mugin. Voluspa, the prophetess . . .

I broke off when I saw a look of genuine fear in Miss Severn's eyes. Hunting for safe topics I spoke once more of the weather. That day was typically overcast and damp. She examined my face quite calmly as I floundered. In desperation I almost began discussing the pursuit of ignoble success, crass material success, for which I considered Warwick was sacrificing his learning and imaginative gifts.

Instead I said:

— I believe you like boating?

She nodded.

I noticed that before she spoke, she almost always coughed or took a deep breath. And occasionally that she took a deep breath like a sigh but said nothing. She did not appear nervous or under pressure to sustain a conversation. It was left to me to introduce each new subject . . . Warwick and his expertise with a camera . . . The spaniel I regretted not bringing with me . . . My poor eyesight . . . Delicate childhood . . . Educated at home . . .

A change of tone, a sudden decisiveness marked Miss Severn's abrupt announcement that she must be getting back to the house. I offered to walk part of the way with her. With reference to Warwick's engagement to a young lady from Gloucester, Miss Severn recalled that her mother used to know some people from that part of the country. Not surprisingly their names meant nothing to me. Although it was not easy searching for safe ideas, somehow, with occasional assistance from the unresponsive spinster (further brief remarks about her brothers at public school, at Oxford and afterwards), I managed to keep a strained conversation going. The fact that the person I was talking to was the main reason why I had come to Coniston a second time — this was never hinted at. No one listening to us could ever have imagined this was the case.

After one embarrassingly long silence, as we were passing Tent Lodge, Miss Severn remarked:

— I believe you have been talking to Caroline Stalker about me.

— We needed Mrs Rigby's help in our researches, I explained.

— I haven't spoken to Caroline since Mother died, said Miss Severn. Even before then I hardly saw her after she married Daniel Rigby.

— Mrs Rigby speaks very highly of you, I stammered. She has been very helpful to us in our researches.

— When the house is sold and I move into the village, I shall probably call on Caroline, said Miss Severn with comparative animation.

— I'm sure she will be pleased to see you, I effused. She thinks you must be very lonely in the big house.

— Oh, the loneliness doesn't trouble me, Violet said. But I cannot afford the upkeep of the house. Anyway it will be sold soon.

We were drawing near to Brantwood. The taciturn Violet muttered inaudibly, apologies or thanks for escorting her, and ran from me as she had once run from Warwick.

Looking in our direction from the garden at Brantwood was the girl whose name I still didn't know. She wore a white muslin dress and a straw hat. She looked very white-faced and frail. In a basketwork chair just behind her a bearded figure was sitting. Rather inappropriately (even for such a poor summer) the man wore a broad-brimmed dark hat and a heavy overcoat with a cape. He was holding a gnarled walking-stick across his knees. Violet ran to them like a servant who might be scolded for too long an absence. The man did not look like a gardener. He scowled intently, apparently at me, although I have seen that particular expression before on the faces of blind men. I raised my hat to the man and girl. My doing this provoked a disdainful look from the girl. Very likely the heavy, scowling man was the agent for the local auctioneers, in charge of arrangements for the forthcoming sale of Ruskin's letters and personal belongings.

After walking a few yards, I glanced back just as Violet was disappearing indoors. The man and girl must have already gone inside. More and more I tended to the view that Miss Severn was genuinely indifferent to the decay of the estate and relished her freedom there in isolation. She was so uncommonly unsociable for a woman, and perhaps she was attached to the scenes of her early life despite the spectre that had haunted them. The opposite position of course was tenable, I mean that the sale of the house would sever her links with the past and free her from the fears that had dominated her childhood. The hardy recluse had left it very late to begin a totally new life. When she was compelled to leave Brantwood, most likely she would feel disoriented even if also relieved of a responsibility and of burdensome memories.

Two large crows (possibly ravens) croaked and strutted regally in a field between the road and the lake. Out on the lake a sail quivered with 'a fretful flutter . . . like a man in a fever fit'. That was how Ruskin had described the sail of

97

Arthur Severn's boat seen from his study windows fifty years before.

A letter from Warwick, briefer, and more restrained and serious than usual (except for one page), reached me the day following my meeting with Violet Severn. Warwick asked me not to fill my letters in future with journalistic dross. (I had mentioned a road accident I had witnessed involving a child.) What he expected from me, Warwick wrote, was: 'the ignes-fatui or the corpse-light flickering above the decomposing body of that extinct religion of art, of which you are perhaps the last crazy votary. Either that or an anatomy of the politics of sitting still in a corner like Jack Horner, with your treasured brand of inwardness sealed in an air-tight preserves-jar . . .' More realistically he said he would be satisfied with the latest news of the fiendish landlady with the black battle-plan on her face. *

In my reply I described the encounter by the lake with the châtelaine of Brantwood, but in rather a perfunctory fashion. For after all, what had that meeting amounted to? A polite exercise in avoiding the one subject I was anxious to discuss with her. A ritual parley in which nothing relevant was discussed. Miss Severn had not taken immediate flight but was the likelihood of a real interview at a later date appreciably greater?

That particular letter to Warwick incorporated a lengthy passage on the landlady and three of her friends engaged in a game of bagatelle. It was based on a glimpse I had had one afternoon on my way upstairs, of Mrs Elms brandishing a bagatelle cue as she and her companions avidly followed the progress of the steel ball down the board to its modest appointment with destiny i.e. the various numbered rewards, the cups, the small triangles, the larger and smaller

---

* 'The black battle-stain on a soldier's face is not vulgar, but the dirty face of a housemaid is' — *Modern Painters*, V.

round compounds enclosed by palisades of tiny nails . . . The other players, the women I had previously referred to as Furies in my letters, I re-named Norns. I struck out a comparison between the landlady and the Midgard serpent, afraid that this facetious episode might (serpent-like) devour the entire letter. To be honest I exaggerated (perhaps I even invented) the look of exultation or rapacity that transfigured the landlady's gaunt features as she leaned over the master board. This image certainly had none of the tenacious disturbing power (the circumstances in no way comparable) that belong to the Sunday morning when I stood in the doorway of the living-room, terrified and hypnotized by the forbidden sight of the priestess or prophetess as she gazed into the speckled mirror to draw out an enormous hatpin from a maroon cloche-hat.

I made the most of the bagatelle incident but it was trivial by comparison.

I signed off with regards to the fiancée.

One afternoon, reading through the transcriptions of interviews in my notebooks, it occured to me that if I made the effort to call once more on the Rigbys, at least I might be able to add to my notes of the reminiscences of Ruskin's valet, Peter Baxter.

I had allowed more than a fortnight to go by since I had spoken to Violet Severn. I attributed my inactivity to a conscious design of lying low. I argued that I was giving her time to grow accustomed to the idea that I was in the neighbourhood again. Looking back, there seems little to justify this view of the situation. But it proved extraordinarily difficult to overcome the habits of sloth and mournful passivity that had gained the upper hand since my arrival at Coniston.

Following my encounter with Miss Severn it rained continuously for days. Even after the rain had temporarily spent itself, the weather was chilly and overcast or misty, the hills two-thirds erased, the nodding slatternly leaf-heavy trees as ugly as giant-headed cabbages, the red roses on garden trellises bulging shapelessly, in disorder, deprived of their real texture and colour, mere emblems of summer, in abject subjection to the shabby or thundery grey of the sky and the obtrusive green of the rank sodden grass, the oversized sycamore and other leaves, and the ferns . . .

I told myself that I would recover a sense of purpose and urgency as the time of the sale of the remaining treasures at Brantwood drew nearer.

It was an effort to go out and see the Rigbys.

In their small, tidy front garden were a rose bush, geraniums, London Pride, a miniature rockery, and ferns that brushed against my legs as I stooped to unlatch the little gate. A tortoise-shell cat lay sleeping on a low wall.

I thought I would find one or another of the Rigbys at home. Some time passed before anyone came to the door but I did not seriously imagine they would have left Mrs Rigby's bedridden mother alone. It was a dismal afternoon, with more rain threatening. A sop of mist half concealed a horned crag. The Old Man was brooding and dark.

Both husband and wife were at home. They seemed genuinely pleased to see me again. Nothing in their circumstances had apparently changed since I saw them last. And they showed less surprise than I expected that I had come on my own on a second visit to Coniston. If Mrs Rigby had seen me recently in the village, she did not embarrass me by mentioning it.

It was not long before it became obvious there was little extra to be learned, at least not about the valet's account of the Sandgate months.

— Mr Ruskin would go to a hotel for his meals, Mr Rigby recalled. He ate well. Then back he went to the sea-front cottage. Peter said he would gaze for hours at the waves without speaking. And when he was busy writing, poor Peter might have been a hundred miles away. He said the

Master used to stare fixedly at him, pen in hand, without seeing him. By contrast, in the last years at Brantwood, Peter said it was heartbreaking to see him at his desk unable to write.

Mr Rigby did remember some more about the great man's health that I thought I might be able to use. About his physical health. Although for a man of his years the Master's eyesight was good, he complained of floating threads and even sparks before his eyes. And there was a hissing in his ears that he compared to the hiss of the serpent in the garden of Eden.

— I told you before, he said, that the Master used to describe his dreams. One of them was a dream of a hog-faced woman. Caroline reminded me of this not long ago when we were talking of the old days.

— A hog-faced woman with an ingratiating manner and a really captivating voice, said his wife.

— That's right, said Mr Rigby. And suddenly out of the mouth of the hog-faced woman came the most frightful snake-hissing. When the Master woke up of course the hissing was still there. The hissing in his ears. Peter told me that syringing did them no good. The noise was so loud at times, the Master said he could distinguish it from the crash of breakers on the shore. It made itself heard in all but the very strongest of winds.

I told them I would make a note of the hog-faced woman/snake dream. I was sure I hadn't come across that particular dream anywhere in the diaries.

Mr Rigby began to talk again about the time Baxter had panicked when he had been out all afternoon with his lady friend and had come back to find Ruskin unconcerned about the passage of time . . .

— And the strange thing he said about his books, said Mr Rigby, being like dead things on the wall.

— Yes, I said, I made a note of that before.

— Did you write down what Peter said? Peter had the presence of mind to suggest that a book comes to life when you open it and begin to read. But the Master wouldn't be comforted. He said something about so much of a man's brain work being useless.

— Something very similar is recorded in the diaries, I told them. 'How great a quantity of brain-motion is utterly useless.'

Mrs Rigby had heard a humorous story about when the Master gave a friend the choice of one or another of his Turner watercolours as a present and the friend had said 'One good Turner deserves another' and he got both for his cheek.

Mr Rigby said:

— Peter used to tell me about the Master trying to dance the 'Perfect Cure' while dressing. A more ludicrous sight would be hard to imagine.

Compared with my unpleasant lodgings it was very agreeable sitting in the living-kitchen of the Rigbys cottage. But I soon realized there was little extra information about Ruskin to be hoped for. To help the conversation along I mentioned the prowler. The local newspaper, in which for so long there had been no mention of him, had begun to show an interest. I asked the Rigbys if they knew what exactly it was the prowler had done.

— Oh, stolen a chicken now and then perhaps, said Mrs Rigby, and frightened a few giddy girls and old maids. Given people the opportunity to enjoy being frightened.

— You don't take it seriously then? I said.

— As far as one can tell, said Daniel Rigby, he is simply a peeping Tom. Why there should be a fuss in this particular case is beyond me. I don't believe he has actually *done* anything.

— You'll have to watch out if you intend spending much time around Brantwood, his wife said to me with a smile. The prowler has been seen on the East Lake road.

— You mean I might be in some danger?

The couple smiled broadly.

— You mean I might be mistaken for him?

— My wife was only teasing you, sir, said Mr Rigby. You could never be mistaken for the prowler. He is reckoned to be quite an elderly man, heavily built, with a beard. Like Landru.

— You can tell it is a to-do about nothing, said Mrs Rigby, by the fact that it is not the farmers' wives and girls in the isolated places that are causing such a commotion — it is the women here in the village who are obsessed by the prowler although no one I have spoken to has actually seen him. I thought Violet would laugh outright when I mentioned him.

— Violet Severn has been to see you! I exclaimed.

— Yes. She has been here twice in the last fortnight. Before that it was almost ten years since we had a real conversation.

I told Mrs Rigby about my encounter with Violet Severn down by the lake. I repeated the gist of our conversation. Mrs Rigby thanked me for my apparent success in getting Violet to look up one of her old friends.

— She never said a word about having spoken to you, though, she said. But your mentioning me to her must have made her realize she still has friends in the village. And yet she is one who has walked right past me more than once in the last twelve months.

— Is she definitely moving to the village? I hastened to ask.

— She says she will as soon as the house is sold. There is a buyer interested she says. But first there is the sale of the things that haven't been disposed of already. Letters and odds and ends.

They asked where I was staying. Was I staying at The Sun Inn like last time? I told them I was lodging with a Mrs Elms. I admitted I was far from happy there. The couple knew Mrs Elms. She had the reputation of being a dragon. Mrs Rigby suggested some reasonably priced lodgings where I would be more comfortable and made very welcome. If the cottage had been bigger and there hadn't been Mrs Rigby's invalid mother upstairs, I could have stayed with them. I thanked her but I said I would probably not remain very long after the Brantwood sale. I thought I could survive Mrs Elms's cooking and overbearing manner till then.

— I expect she still has soot on her face during the week and wears rouge on Sunday for church, said Daniel Rigby, smiling.

— I haven't seen Gladys Elms for a long time, said his wife. I thought she didn't take in lodgers any more.

Mrs Rigby waited until her husband had gone out for some tobacco to tell me she was very worried about Violet Severn.

— She should have got right away from that house years ago. She has become strange living there so cut off from everybody. It's thirty years since Mr Ruskin died yet she still feels his presence there she tells me. And she is frightened of him still.

— I would very much like to speak to her about Ruskin, I said.

Mrs Rigby shook her head.

— I don't think she will ever speak to you on that subject. Not when she knows it's for your book. And you can hardly pretend it isn't now. Violet seems to hate books and writers because of the old man. She talks about her childhood as though it were yesterday. When she started reminiscing I encouraged her at first, but I have decided it's not encouragement she needs.

— Perhaps Miss Severn should have written her memoirs. To get it out of her system, I said.

— You know she claims she still sees him. At times she sees him at the window looking in at her.

Taken aback, I gazed at Mrs Rigby, possibly open-mouthed.

— Yes, Mrs Rigby continued. She says she sees him regularly. He looks at her, she says, with a meaning she can't understand. When she used to describe him spying on her, when she was a girl, she always said he had a vacant look on his face.

— Did she tell you anything else?

— She mostly spoke about the house going to rack and ruin and how she is dreading the sale. She was very defensive about the state of the house. She said it's not a sin to let a house go to rack and ruin. After all, it is not her house and she has not the means to improve it . . . She was very agitated at times. I am very worried about her.

— Did she say anything else about Ruskin looking in at her?

— Yes. I am afraid she did. She said he sometimes looks at her with a mocking, sneering expression. At other times he appears to be blowing on the glass although the pane doesn't cloud over.

— She only sees him like that, looking at her from outside through the window?

— As far as I know. Yes. She says he is not just looking at *her*. He looks beyond and above her, too, at the walls, the furnishings . . . I haven't told anyone about this, not even my husband. I don't want word to get around that poor Violet is deranged. People think anyone as self-sufficient as Violet has been is bound to be rather peculiar but I think she is generally respected as a hardy sort of woman. And, after all, she *is* the last link with the old days at Brantwood. If you do get to see Violet again, you must promise not to mention what I have told you. She asked me not to breathe a word of it to anybody. I am sure you won't use what I have told you for your book.

— Of course not, I assured her, although I had already made notes of a metaphorical spectre haunting Violet Severn.

— She should see a doctor, shouldn't she? I added.

— If I had suggested that, I doubt I would have seen her again. She didn't refer to the subject the second time she came and perhaps she seemed a little less on edge.

105

— It's hard to believe she was serious, I said. The likeliest explanation is that she confuses dreams with reality. The experiences of her childhood must have been exceptionally strong to have had such a long-lasting effect. The sooner she moves from the house the better, I would say.

Mrs Rigby agreed.

— She doesn't drink does she? I asked as an afterthought.

— That never occured to me, said Mrs Rigby. I wouldn't have said so.

— You don't think there is a possibility that it could be the famous Peeping Tom she has seen? The prowler. If he is bearded and elderly she might confuse him with the bogeyman of her childhood.

— Violet laughed to scorn the talk of a prowler.

I mentioned that I had overheard an elderly man in the village claim the prowler resembled old Mr Ruskin.

— That doesn't surprise me, Mrs Rigby said. People of my generation and older were either afraid of him or sorry for him or both. Even Daniel says he was a little afraid of him. That is why I can understand very well Violet being terrified as a child . . . Violet doesn't believe she is seeing a ghost. Or a real person. She believes it is all in her imagination. In my opinion that doesn't make it any easier for her.

— I would like to speak to her again, I said. Should I write first or just call?

— I can't advise you there, said Mrs Rigby. If it was just a matter of a social call I would say yes but Violet is too mistrustful of young gentlemen like you and your cousin to help you, in my opinion.

— I must try one last time, I said. I shall write to her and hope to change her mind.

Mrs Rigby considered I would be wasting my time. And she was very anxious that I shouldn't upset her old friend when she was already so disturbed.

— What is the gardener at Brantwood like? I asked as I was leaving.

Mr Rigby had appeared at the end of the street and was waving to us.

She didn't know the gardener or his family at all really. I had meant what was he like in appearance. Mrs Rigby thought I was inquiring about his manner and character. I described the girl my cousin and I had seen with Miss Severn. Mrs Rigby could only assume the girl must be a recent friend of Violet's. She didn't know anyone like my description.

I wrote to Miss Severn and waited a few days. There was no reply. When I called at the house, a little middle-aged woman with a care-lined face and yellow crooked teeth answered the bell. She told me Violet was not at home. 'Violet' not 'Miss Severn' was what she said. She couldn't tell me when she would be in. The woman's voice was brittle; she sounded ill-tempered but this may have been the result of nervousness, especially if Violet was, in fact, somewhere in the house, listening with a door ajar. For a moment I thought I saw an arm signalling from an upstairs window but almost certainly it was the reflection of a branch I saw. The day was fine but breezy.

In my 'workroom' I put up two pictures: one a lithograph by Odilon Redon, To Gustave Flaubert, 1889, *Death: my irony surpasses all others*; the other I had cut out of the *Studio* magazine — it depicted a double row of leafless fastigiate trees suspended upside down from a staring white ceiling in a room where a gentleman with a pencil-line moustache on a smug prismoidal face was reading by a small fireplace. There was a pulley next to the hanging trees of the kind that operates those clothes-rails that can be lowered from a ceiling.

These pictures I put up to confront the framed oleographs of sunsets over lakes and mountains. The landlady's cada-verous face appeared round the door as I was tacking up the second of the pictures. There was a dirty mark on her right cheek, another at her temple almost hidden by strands of grey, maenad hair. I was startled: the drawing-pin fell from my grasp; the surrealist illustration slipped to the floor.

— I didn't hear you come in, muttered the landlady.

She padded away down the lobby towards the kitchen.

I mouthed curses slowly, soundlessly, into a small looking-glass on the mantlepiece. The looking-glass misted over and I became aware of a turbaned figure watching me from outside the ashpit and privy doors in the narrow, flagged backyard.

I never seriously entertained the idea that Violet Severn might have fled from her 'apparition' at Brantwood, any more than I gave serious consideration to the theory that someone was dressing up as the dead writer to frighten Violet out of her inheritance. (I assumed that some of the proceeds of the eventual sale of the house would go to the youngest daughter.) What Mrs Rigby had told me added a little to my knowledge of Violet but not of Ruskin. Could I make use of Violet? I saw the unattractive, weather-browned spinster as the medium. With her help as intermediary could I establish contact with *him*? This fanciful idea both attracted me and repelled me, but the practicalities involved in getting Violet to co-operate seemed insuperable.

I called at Brantwood next day. Miss Severn was in London I was now told. Quite plausible. Legal business. Financial matters. A man I had never seen before, who looked like a gardener, told me this. I was not totally convinced and looked out across the lake for a sail or a rowboat. I could only see the Victorian steamboat tied up at the main landing-stage. A seagull overhead cried harshly; another farther away seemed to answer it. ('Not the common shrieking gull, but one that gives a low, clear, plaintive whistle of two short notes, dying on the wind like a far away human voice.')

Further attempts to see Violet Severn met with no success. Once the preparations had begun for the three-day sale I was reluctant to be seen hanging about the place. In a final message handed in at the door I made an embarrassingly emotional appeal for Violet's help in my researches. Like my previous notes and letters it was disregarded.

If I am to believe the landlady, during one of my fruitless trips to Brantwood, I had a female caller. The description did not fit Violet Severn or anyone else I knew at Coniston. The visitor had left no name. When I asked Mrs Elms exactly what my caller had said to her, the landlady chose to be deaf. She appeared to believe that I knew very well who the young woman was and was impatient with me for continuing to feign ignorance.

EIGHT

As I came down the stairs on the final day of the Brantwood
sale, the landlady was in conversation with one of her cronies
on the front step. The faces of both women froze when
they saw me. The never-ending tap of their speech froze also.

— A wet day, I remarked.

It seemed as if neither of them was going to speak. This
could only be explained by a fixed animosity to me. (It was at
that moment that I made my decision to leave Coniston that
afternoon or, at the latest, evening.) The landlady's friend in
fact did speak. She pointed across the street to a grotesque,
six-foot tall, beshawled, bedraggled woman with red hair
and a brick-red face, who could have been mistaken for a
pantomime dame.

— Here's one you should talk to. Mr Ruskin's pet, she
said.

Both women laughed, apparently at my expense as well as
that of the bizarre-looking female who was striding past.

— She'll be in a hurry to buy back her old love letters, Mrs
Elms said loudly. Ask her why Violet Severn is never lonely!

To their evident delight my way (initially) lay in the same
direction as that of the red-haired female Grenadier.

At the main steamer pier, steamerless just then and
otherwise quite deserted, I watched gulls and coots in among
the reeds and out on the lake. Gulls moved gently on the
water like paper boats. Fussily energetic and self-assertive,
coal-black coots with their white chamfron above the white
beak, made short sharp 'SKIK' noises, striking their flints
that never catch fire. Approaching from the opposite bank,

from 'Joanna's Bay', a rowboat came near enough for me to identify two female figures; the older woman at the oars I imagined might be Violet Severn. Mrs Rigby had told me that Violet Severn had been out rowing on the lake the day her 89-year-old father was buried in London. What more natural than that now she should make her escape from the invaders of her privacy, the vultures that descend on the decaying carcass of an old house, picking from its old bones the flesh, the few sticks of furniture, the fabrics, the old clothes, the old papers, the old unmarketable pictures, the old utensils, the old forgeries! . . .

Violet had been nowhere in sight on the first day of the sale. Yesterday and the day before I had spent indoors, writing and appraising the value of what I had purchased then.

The sale had not yet started its final day when I came to Brantwood. I walked past the house to Beck Leven and to Fir Island. It was drizzling. From the shore I saw the rowboat again. The female at the oars I was certain was Violet Severn. Seated facing her was the bulky figure of a man. For a moment, forgetting the sale at Brantwood was due to Mr Severn's demise, I thought that might be Mr Severn in the boat with her.

When the sale resumed, it was raining rather harder. The sale was held in the garden. I wondered if Collingwood would be there, his son or his daughter. I saw no one I had ever spoken to before. Some faces were vaguely familiar. On the opening day of the sale I had acquired a lace handkerchief, a blue stock and a stockinet nightcap belonging to the great man. There seemed to be more neatly-tied, rainspattered bundles of paper on this, the last day, than on the 28th. I knew that in retrospect I would be amazed at my indifference. A kind of indecisiveness and apathy overcomes me on such occasions. There were few signs of any exceptional interest in the faces of buyers and bystanders. I heard an American accent — a well-dressed silver-haired man wearing rimless glasses. I had to force myself not to walk away empty handed. I heard afterwards that some letters and MSS. that had remained unsold had been burned. If I had read this in a book, it would have seemed inconceivable, sacrilegious. At the time, in my state of apathy, of extremely low vitality, if the diaries had been available still for auction and my means had been greater, I might have felt too listless even to bid for them.

The fate of Brantwood reminded me of the fate of Flaubert's Croisset, similarly dilapidated before it was sold to a distiller. I thought of Henry James's portrait of Flaubert at Croisset. An immobile god in a petrified landscape. I had read somewhere a whimsical analogy between the fate of Croisset, ivory tower replaced by a distillery, and the fate of Emma Bovary's daughter, Berthe, heiress to romantic dreams, doomed to a life of hardship, inescapable dull sordid routine in a cotton mill. I hoped someone would buy Brantwood and restore it to its former condition. If my cousin had been with me he could have taken pictures of the house and grounds at their most neglected. The tennis lawn, where Ruskin had put the players off their game, had reverted to rough meadow. Joan's garden: a wilderness of nettles. The house had perhaps not deteriorated so very obviously from the outside but the end of July was dark and rainy and the sale added finality to the melancholy spectacle of its decay.

'Dark — dark — with rain' the day was.

On my way back to the village I walked through muddy fields to Tent Lodge. Sheep ran away at my approach. I saw the *Gondola* on the murky lake. When my path rejoined the road, a black limousine coming from the direction of Brantwood, silently coasted round the bend. I stepped back against a window of Tent Cottage while it passed. So heavily veiled she looked to be blindfolded, a fat woman in black bombazine sat alone in the back seat. The big car, travelling slowly, seemed to be coming to a halt. I had the grotesque notion that I was going to be offered a lift. I raised my hat and, half turning, was startled by eyes above the net of the cottage window very close to mine.

When the car containing the stout veiled woman in black had rounded the next bend, absolute peace returned to the narrow lakeside road. Immediately the car had gone, a squirrel came down from a tree and scampered along the low wall that surrounds the property of Tent Lodge. The drizzle was turning to rain.

When the misty lake came into view again I decided I would take shelter in the rustic avenue of overarching trees that leads to a short pier on the north-east bank.

It troubled me, my failure to transform the day into a historic event. For my failure to rise to the occasion, I blamed the mediocre, bored people at the sale and the Scotch mist that blurred every vista. Most of all however I blamed my physical state: a bilious disorder causing listlessness and mental puzzlement, the cumulative effect of greasy breakfasts and unappetizing suppers. In particular, to last night's tough veal cutlets I attributed my heavy head, my weariness, a sense of darkness in my brains . . . Very soft and peaceful by the water. Wavelets lapping. Refreshing! A possibility that the heaviness of the day might yet lighten. Instead, quite suddenly, with finality, the day darkened. I won't indulge in description of a scene that the great Describer, Scourge and Seer, has described with savage precision. Rain fell. The soft air was transformed into a malignant chill. In my sounding-box of trees I was perfectly dry, but out there, at the very end of the brown rain-washed planks of the jetty (I remembered it as silvered by rime during our winter visit) a man was standing. Water gushed from the sloping brim of his large hat as if from a waterspout. The heavily-built man wore a long overcoat with a cape, no waterproof. Why did he remain there? Wishing to be alone, I walked back towards the road. I should add that it was not merely the wish to be alone that influenced me. It was also embarrassment. To stay close to the jetty with the spectacle before me of a man deliberately getting himself soaked was embarrassing. It was his own business. If he had chosen to stand on his head out there at the end of the double rows of trees, it was his own business. A man of mature years, heavily built, unusually long hair visible beneath his hat. To call out to him to come in under the shelter of the trees would have put him and myself out of countenance. An impertinent, unwarranted intrusion! On the other hand if my concern was unresented or positively welcomed, a tedious conversation would inevitably follow. Involvement of some kind. That was the last thing I wanted before my imminent departure. To listen to some pathetic story, some personal tragedy even! He enraged me. I never helped lame dogs. I was not going to start with him.

The thought that this might be the famous prowler never entered my head.

A couple of motor cars swished past along the road to the village. A group on foot went by with umbrellas. I gazed out at the rain from my snug bower. More cars passed. A languid susurration. I retraced my steps under the noisy, sheltering canopy to the jetty. The rain fell as relentlessly; the same overlapping circles eternally formed on the surface of the water, but of the thick-set, grey-haired figure on the steamer jetty there was, rather mysteriously, no sign.

Since leaving the Brantwood sale, I had been preoccupied by the thought that the project my cousin and I had set out to accomplish two years before could never be completed successfully and that to continue alone along these lines would merely create an ever-increasing distance between myself and my subject, as though I were digging a deeper and deeper hole with the insane intention of digging my way to a superior vantage point. Not that any better alternatives presented themselves to me! A fictional treatment would satisfy neither the discriminating reader nor this writer. It seemed nothing short of some mediumistically-arranged contact with our subject, telepathy with the dead

114

(intercession by the Powers on High, the stones of Brant-wood and — possibly — the spinster who refused to see me), could provide the intimate knowledge I had once dreamed of attaining so simply through the memories of friends.

At last, braving the rain that showed no sign of slackening, I returned to my lodgings. I packed my things. My landlady was out. Normally I would have paid my last respects to the bleak little room at the back of the Institute, the cold narrow confines to which Fame and Genius had shrunk, but I was afraid of lingering in the village because I was terrified I might run into Mrs Elms. The money I had left for her in an envelope would not compensate her for the damage I had caused moments before leaving the empty house. Prompted by I don't know what devil, I had shattered the tarnished over-mantel mirror with a paperweight — the same living-room mirror in the depths of which the landlady had contemplated her image as she drew out the enormous hatpin with the solemnity and sense of ritual of a priestess. On the main journey south I was full of contrition, or of self-pity at the trouble I might have brought upon myself. It was a cold, rainy, stormy evening. At the junction where I had an hour's wait to connect with the London train, whenever the sounds of the wind gusting subsided, I could hear a wild ringing and clanking and greedy swilling down a thousand sink-holes, a universal draining, then a prolonged grating, with shudder-ing, sometimes reedy, sometimes ferruginous moans; over-head, swinging nameboards creaked and squealed; and above the next platform, after the departure of a local train, a white sea bird, glimpsed among the foul smoke-shreds carried up to the glass roof, brought to mind the landlady's pale face marked with soot and ashes, implacably vengeful, forever pursuing me; — a whey-faced fury she had pursued me there out of the storm and darkness.

My departure (always to be associated with my act of vandalism) marked the beginning of the end of the project.

115

It seemed extremely unlikely that I would ever return to Coniston.

Waiting for me at home was a letter addressed to Warwick and myself from Lanehead, the house I had deliberately stayed away from while in Coniston, although there is no doubt I would have received a cordial welcome if I had roused myself to call on the old man.

The handwriting was Collingwood's daughter's. The brief letter conveyed general good wishes to us both from father and daughter. They were surprised not to have heard anything more of our interesting Ruskin project. Did we know about the sale of the remaining Ruskin relics due to be held at Brantwood at the end of the month? (The envelope was postmarked early July.)

There were two enclosures. One was Warwick's picture postcard of Coniston Water from Brantwood. Barbara Gnosspelius had seen it in a village shop. I had grown used to seeing it during my second stay in Coniston. After Warwick's apostasy I regarded the card, to say the least, with mixed feelings. Collingwood had scrawled 'Congratulations. Marvellous photograph' on the back.

The more significant enclosure was a second letter — from the United States, from the American graduate scholar, Helen Gill Viljoen. This also proved to be largely concerned with the sale at Brantwood, the gist being that if we were going to attend the sale, would we let her know if anything unexpected and exceptional came under the hammer? She wished it was possible for her just then to visit England. She had the warmest of memories of a cold English winter in spite of the personal distress she was experiencing at the time. (When we learned from Collingwood that she was in the process of getting a divorce, Warwick had murmured to me that *that* must be the cause of her high spirits.) Mrs Viljoen maintained that she often thought of her time at How Head

Farm and at Brantwood, of Mrs Cowman, of kind old Mr Collingwood and poor dear funny Violet.

Warwick had always insisted that the American's high spirits were not simply an expression of natural Yankee exuberance (and not seriously the prospect of liberation from her husband), but that she had chanced upon some valuable discovery. Possibly she had made off with some unknown treasure long overlooked in Ruskin's library but it seemed more likely that she had copied out something of importance that we had missed. When we had first heard that Violet Severn was kindly disposed towards the American, we had speculated on the possibility of her being shown some secret cache of documents and keepsakes that had been preserved over the years well away from the burrowing snouts of scholars. Letters perhaps. Surviving love-letters not for the eyes of 'cockney' historians. A secret journal? Violet's friendliness towards Mrs Viljoen had been in such marked contrast to her treatment of us that we thought she must have been quite infatuated with the personality of the younger woman, envying her her independent spirit, confidence, enthusiasm, liveliness, sense of purpose, and utter freedom from any morbid subjection to the past.

Compared with Helen Viljoen we had spent little time within the walls of Brantwood. What time we had spent there had been on sufferance, made possible only through Collingwood's good offices. The material we had studied most, during our stay in the unpicturesque mining village, we had removed temporarily to our lodgings with Collingwood's permission and Violet's tacit approval — or even (who knows?) her positive encouragement since it had meant there was less risk of running into us by accident.

'Les Frères Zemgano', the American began her letter.

I didn't suppose she imagined we would still be at Coniston but Collingwood was her only means of contacting us. It was a great pity the letter had not been sent on to me. But I had seen nothing offered for sale that I would have described as exciting or exceptional. I did not reply to the letter. At the time I could not bear to dwell on the possibility that the Bluestocking from across the Atlantic had made some momentous discovery with or without the help of Violet Severn. Years afterwards I was still scanning academic literary journals, dreading that I might come across an article that would totally transform attitudes to Ruskin, heralding vast future productions perhaps, by the same pen, grown from the seeds of whatever it was that Mrs Viljoen had stumbled upon or had revealed to her that winter in the Lake District.

I forwarded both letters to Warwick. He accepted them without comment. Not long afterwards he let me have his Ruskin notes. I could use them or destroy them as I thought fit. As well as the notes there was miscellaneous material: pamphlets, guides, photographs.

Among the photographs were some he had taken in Coniston in the winter of 1929, landscapes except for one that caused me some consternation. This was a full-length portrait of the nameless young friend of Violet Severn, the girl we had seen beating dusty hassocks outside the village church, the girl I had seen more recently with an elderly man in the village and in the garden at Brantwood. Warwick's picture had been taken somewhere by Coniston Water.

The existence of the photograph proved that Warwick had met the girl somewhere on his own and persuaded her to pose for him. I never received a satisfactory explanation how this had happened and how intimate their friendship had been.

— How can you be intimate with a dryad, an undine or naiad? had been Warwick's facetious comment.

Despite the rigours of a Lakeland winter, in the photograph the girl is wearing neither hat nor coat; her expression is unsmiling, or perhaps she is faintly smiling, the lips hesitating whether to smile or not, the eyes remaining melancholy and cold; in the background the lake can be glimpsed, there are frost-whitened trees, the planks of a jetty are also silvered with frost, as I remembered the landing-stage at Monk Coniston . . . Some slight defects on the photograph Warwick could not account for; he had made a note to that effect on the back. No name with the snapshot. When I pressed him about this he maintained he had no more information about the girl — about her name, age, status, parentage, relationship to Violet Severn and to Brantwood — than I had.

Among the scribbled notes that Warwick sent to me, one brief paragraph compared Ruskin's dream, recorded in the diaries, of an injured man crawling *towards* a great fire with the case of the fire at the Colney Hatch lunatic asylum that occured three years after Ruskin's death, in which many extra lives were lost because patients, after being dragged out by their heroic rescuers, had rushed back into the blazing building. Many of Warwick's notes were of that kind, mildly interesting but not really usable and undermined by whimsy and often by quite absurd speculations or comments. For instance, a footnote to that particular note queried: 'A case of Bovarysme?'

One paragraph proclaimed, as if based on factual research, that each major manufacturing town in the north boasts 'at least three undesirable residences in the suburbs called Brantwood with turrets much larger than the original, laurelled drives, stained-glass in all the windows, conservatories, "damp-souled" housemaids, and shrivelled prune-shaped electric light-fittings in masque of the red death vestibules.' Included, in an apparently serious and comprehensive list of the food and drink that Ruskin had recorded in various parts of his diaries as giving rise to his bilious dreams, were some blatantly spurious items such as Martinmas goose, Madagascar meat-balls and potted crocodile. The most irrelevant note was a description of Holman Hunt's house in Kensington resembling a hospital for tropical diseases.

119

A single reference that must have been to the girl on the snapshot came at the end of a page of Ruskin notes. It read: 'Girl. Unknown. Consumptive.' And, in quotation marks, a phrase that seemed wildly inappropriate if it was still the girl that was meant: 'A tendency to corporeal degradation.'

Something about the frail appearance and the almost-despairing expression in the eyes of the girl in the snapshot made me think of the pathetic letter written by Rose La Touche to Joan Severn, on a train journey to Holyhead and her home in Ireland (Harristown) not many months before her early death: 'Somehow a blight seems to have got at the very stalk of my life and I shall never grow out of it.'

Warwick's covering letter contained the last written remarks he made to me on the subject of Ruskin and my fiasco of a second visit to Coniston. He considered that I had lost the battle to penetrate more deeply into the mystery of Ruskin's last years for the same reason that the popular press used to say that Germany had lost the Great War — because of Teutonic grim humourlessness and associated depression, leading ultimately to a total loss of morale.

For a long time I was convinced that criminal proceedings would be brought against me for breaking the landlady's mirror. I was relieved when no specific retribution ensued. Strangely enough, for the first few nights after leaving Coniston, I woke to an aural hallucination that Mrs Elms was murmuring my name with endearments, and even moaning softly the other side of my bedroom door. (In my waking hours I regularly pictured the star-shattered mirror, reflecting the landlady with a ferocious expression on her soot-blackened face, bagatelle 'smiting rod' in her hand, and I distinctly heard her venomously articulated syllables threatening a terrible vengeance.)

As they say, dreams go by contraries . . .

It was only the peculiar overpowering sense of heaviness that I felt (my head in particular seemed encased in lead), and

120

an uncanny atmosphere, that reassured me the sounds dying away could be relegated to the same category of experience that Warwick used to describe when he said he sometimes woke in the night, as if disturbed by a fire-bell or a peal of thunder, to an awesome voice addressing him from his father's bedroom. Although greatly distorted, Warwick had no difficulty in recognizing it as his feared and hated headmaster father's 'assembly' voice, reverberant and yet hoarse, with its unmistakable timbre of iron coated with iron filings, uttering indistinct words like some dark tower ogre with a grotesque and terrible slowness.

I did not mention the incident of the mirror to Warwick or to anyone else. It was so out of character that I could scarcely believe I had actually thrown the paperweight. It was even more bizarre than that some kind of relationship, however slight and brief, had existed between Warwick and the consumptive-looking 'Brantwood' girl and that I had been unaware of it. I would never have imagined Warwick could be attracted to such a pale, flat-chested, sickly waif as that girl. I would have said that, for my cousin, a tender friendship with the spectral princess of lakeside and glen was almost as inconceivable as the development of a genuine romantic attachment to the plain, graceless, middle-aged châtelaine of the tower herself. And what had made the situation all the more mysterious had been the fact that I could have counted on the fingers of one hand the number of occasions when either Warwick or I had set out from The Sun Inn without the other during our stay.

In time, long after the threat of some kind of punishment for breaking the landlady's mirror had faded away altogether, I came to regard it almost as a heroic action or gesture — as heroic an action, anyway, as I was capable of. That autumn I spent a few weeks in Innsbruck and northern Italy. (The only continental holiday I was able to afford between the wars.) Mussolini's Italy. However my gaze was fixed exclusively on the past. I explored Ruskin's Venice, Verona, Assisi, Florence, Turin. From a castled crag north of Riva I looked down on a radiant landscape of vines, Lake Garda beyond, and with no skeletons to mar my appreciation of the view. One large bare room in this castle contained only a table, a dusty pen and ink-bottle and the visitor's book. I signed myself John Ruskin.* Had I written Goethe, the name would have been struck out in outrage by the next German visitor, but Ruskin had made no impact on the consciousness of Italians and to his own countrymen he was a mildewy Victorian. Goethe, by contrast, was a name to conjure with in guidebooks. German tourists still followed in his footsteps . . . In Venice, from the campanile of St Mark's, I looked out over the islands in the lagoon and also down at the great square, as though, like Ruskin in his dream, I was straining for a glimpse of Rose La Touche, where she said she would be standing, on that 'level field of chequered stones'. In the shadow of one of the Scaliger castles, in a small north Italian town that for once had no Ruskin associations that I knew of, I came across the twin of Mrs Elms's tarnished overmantel mirror before it was shattered by the paperweight. The mirror was leaning against the wall of a house beneath a shuttered window. A middle-aged grinning Italian kept thrusting back in front of this mirror a shambling fawn-coloured mongrel puppy, frightened and confused at seeing its double and irritated and snappish through rough handling, for the benefit of two gaunt, masculine-looking, white-haired Englishwomen, who were gazing at the man rather than his dog with expressions of horror and scorn, while the deluded man possibly expected the impromptu entertainment he was providing to earn him a few lire.

The postcards and letters I sent to friends and relatives

---

*In a space left on an earlier page I also signed myself Giovanni Rusconi, after the Renaissance architect and near name-sake of Ruskin, commended by him for opposing the plan to rebuild the Doge's Palace.

from Austria and Italy caused some concern. So, at any rate, I discovered later.

I confess there was a feverish, phantasmagoric quality about that Italian holiday. Despite their vivid colours, the images those weeks furnished me with are as unreal, in their way, as the spectral, flickering images of Venice that Warwick and I had seen at the film show at the church hall in Coniston. And yet I would not have said that my state of mind was excessively morbid or irrational. On the other hand, I had been in the grip of my Ruskin obsession for so long that I probably failed to notice the stages by which it deepened and developed and grew more noticeable to others, exerting an influence over a wider and wider area of my life. Long before my second visit to Coniston Warwick's advice to me had been to put the project aside for ten years.

While I was in Italy I had several vivid dreams. The one I remember in most detail dated from the first night I spent in Verona. After an exhausting day's sightseeing — the arena, Can Grande's castle, the church of San Zeno Maggiore, the square of the patricians, Ruskin's view from Fra Giocondo's bridge towards the mountains of Garda — the dream took me far from my immediate surroundings back to the dark, damp, chilly, misty Coniston of the final day of the sale at Brantwood, the Lakeland fells invisible, a dirty eraser obliterating the horizon behind every piece of copse and hillock in the middle-distance, every gritstone wall that closed a steeply-rising field . . . After the Brantwood sale I dreamed I had gone to Collingwood's house, where my listless mood was suddenly transformed when old Collingwood told me he had an item of importance to give me, a present from a very important person. As he said this he nodded and smiled roguishly, significantly, at the oddly-shaped package on his desk. And while I waited impatiently for his tedious preamble to end and for the gift to be presented to me, smoke began pouring out of it — a brownish-black, woolly, very dense smoke of the kind you

123

would see billowing above a blaze at a tyre factory. Openly cursing the old man for his time-wasting rigmarole, I grabbed at the parcel, pulling desperately at the string, calling out for someone to bring a knife or a pair of scissors, and all the time mocked by an awareness of Collingwood's shoulders heaving in damnable, silent, repressed laughter. When I got the brown paper off at last, what I discovered was a fire-blackened and very small gramophone or replica of a gramophone complete with fire-blackened horn. Next to it stood a soot-covered dog — the dog somewhat larger than the gramophone. After I woke I was slow in making the obvious connection between the dog and the gramophone and the famous trademark of His Master's Voice. I remember that it was not until late in the morning that I recalled the dream. After admiring the Scaligers' tombs, I had been watching a priest unhurriedly extinguishing candles in the small dark church of Santa Maria Antica when the dream came to mind. And no doubt it is significant that a much more esoteric association than the association with a record company label, a Ruskin association, occured to me first — this was his dismissal in *Fors* of an early kind of phonograph as a ghastly attempt to make the dead speak out of barrel organs.

From Italy I returned to Innsbruck and then spent a day and a night at Salzburg before setting off for Ostend. In later years it was not easy to convince myself that I had been on the continent at a time of such awesome political significance. So obsessed had I been with literature and the past that when I searched my memory for choice views of Austria and Germany just before the Third Reich, I had to confess that I recalled no armbands with swastikas, no references to Hitler except in the newspapers (although I did see the word *Juden* scrawled on a tenement wall), and the detail that has survived longest was a childish conceit, totally inauthentic. On the way back through Germany the train had halted at a station that looked brand-new, the lamps on the platform were of an advanced design and, as we pulled away, they resembled arms lifted in the Nazi salute to our departing train . . . There was a soldier with a rifle in the corridor. I had not enough experience of Germany and foreign travel to judge whether that was unusual. In the night I was kept awake by the taste of butter biscuits. Feeling unbearably hot, I threw my travelling-rug off and lowered the window. Immediately the short curtains whipped up, struggling wildly until they escaped, streaming like pennants in the night. I kept myself from being sick by breathing in the fresh air slowly and deeply and by fixing my gaze on the horizon, according to the standard advice given to sea voyagers. There happened to be a moon, we were passing down the Rhine valley and I gazed at the black, shaggy, vine-covered hills, at the castles in mezzotint silhouette. I was also aware of lights on the river and the lights of cars attempting to keep up with the train on the parallel shore road at a lower level. I expected to be sick crossing the Channel. Inexplicably I wasn't. I slept on the train to London, wakened only when a fellow-traveller, an elderly distinguished-looking man, leaned forward and touched me on the knee; he muttered a few indistinct, possibly foreign words like someone talking in his sleep and then, as I looked in drowsy wonderment back at him, he seemed astonished at himself and acutely embarrassed, and before I was completely awake, without explanation or apology, he had already gone off down the corridor. Warwick and his fiancée were at Victoria to meet the boat train. We had a meal together. I think one of my postcards must have persuaded Warwick — or more likely a relative, or even the Gloucestershire Boadicea, had persuaded him — to check on my state of mind, though nothing of course was said about this. Once or twice, at table, I caught Warwick looking askance at me. His fiancée rarely stopped talking and fussing over me. This was to be our one and only meeting. Her features were too large for her to wear her black hair as short as she did, and although she had beautiful dark eyes, her face was rather masculine and long, big-chinned and flewed, in contrast rather to the statuesque yet delicately pretty girls Warwick had always been attracted to before. Absent-mindedly, as we were standing outside St Pancras later, surrounded by all my luggage, Warwick pulled down the large peak of my new flat cap which was not unlike the white cap the fiancée wore.

— Your cousin's a lamb, she said.

— Cold mutton, said Warwick.

Both were obviously relieved that I seemed normal. Warwick was disappointed that I had seen no brownshirts. I spoke about Italy in a gushing sort of way. Neither Warwick nor I mentioned Ruskin in front of the fiancée.

During these few hours that were to prove almost the last time I saw Warwick, the first and last time that I saw the woman who became his wife soon afterwards, my cousin and I had only a minute or so alone together. This was in the station urinals immediately before the departure of my train. I had wanted to tell him something about the sale at Brantwood, or rather about the strange knowing words — apparently the words of an initiate — that the landlady had uttered as I set out. Also I intended to mention the figures in the rowboats on Coniston Water and the limousine containing the veiled, stout 'Woman in Black' that had passed me on the East Lake road, coming away from the sale. But when I glanced at Warwick's face beneath his fedora there seemed to be already the first faint sketch of a supercilious smile, waiting to curve definitively on those familiar thin lips, and I hadn't the courage to begin.

And besides, what could he have said, any more than what I might have said myself on his behalf, that at this very moment, even in this day and age, there must be elderly Mrs Pipchins by the score, in lustreless, deep, dead, black bombazine being driven slowly along country lanes in limousines and coupées with mud-splashed fenders over sky-reflecting puddles? And if I had described the old man letting himself get thoroughly soaked at the end of a jetty, Warwick would merely have said that was nothing out of the ordinary either — it was the kind of thing the seasoned traveller expects to observe almost daily and immediately consigns to the useless lumber room of life's unaccountable minor oddities and prosaic mysteries. Nothing out of the ordinary. And then perhaps I would have received a little homily about its being high time I abandoned the Creepy and Crepuscular for real life in the present tense, to give up once and for all my futile attempts to pierce the sacred veil. After all, the veil of the woman in black, the literal veil, probably concealed nothing more wonderful than a present-day Mrs Pipchin's hook nose and grey eye or else the gaunt, pale features of another Mrs Elms . . .

In the urinals, when I looked up, I had seen a bird flutter close to the curved glass roof of the station. Warwick had already moved away from the marble stalls and was waiting, his face expressionless, by the exit. Between the moment we had left her with my luggage and the moment we rejoined the fiancée near the barrier — she was standing heavy and dismal-faced until she noticed us — Warwick and I hadn't exchanged a single word. Smiles and meaningless ritual remarks abounded as the two of them helped me settle my belongings in the carriage, Warwick clasping my hand, the fiancée kissing me on the cheek, until the time came for the train to pull away, leaving the engaged couple waving; they turned as one; I saw their backs, the woman's broader than the man's, a moment before they were lost to view.

PART 3

Envoi

'Such a Dead World – of other people's lives and one's
own.'
– John Ruskin, *Diaries*

NINE

The passage of time has made the last day of the Brantwood
sale grow in significance. But I have retained what I believe
to be an accurate awareness of the total lack of significance it
then held for me. The lake, the house, the village, the
miniature cosily-crumpled mountains to the north, always
appeared to me afterwards as half-erased and rain-hatched
vistas, further darkened by my desolate and listless mood
that day. The sale was unarguably historic as an old newsreel
film is historic — even when it fails to convey a sense of
actuality across the years — faded images of what for me
originally lacked vividness. If my own experience could
become reduced to such a dead world that I had no hope of
re-animating, how much more baseless and vainglorious was
my dream of reviving a past not my own! I argued like this
each time I looked back through the pages of my unfinished
monograph.

As to Brantwood itself, I was conscious that my experience of it was restricted to a sort of interregnum, the period
very likely of its greatest decay. Once I had compared the
house to the Arabian palace in a dream of Ruskin's. The keys
of this palace had been crushed to pieces so that no one would
ever get inside it for its treasures. 'It would all moulder into
ruin.' In fact, soon afterwards when a disciple★ purchased the
property, its future re-furbishment and restoration were
assured. The house did not, after all, suffer the pathetic fate
of Flaubert's Croisset — decay — demolition — the

★John Howard Whitehouse bought Ruskin's domain and diaries.

131

distillery. But for me it remained as I had known it, with an ageing spinster for châtelaine, encamped there for some years in the leaky, draughty house like a frail farouche indifferent Goth inhabiting the former centre of a cultural empire.

When I read the *Times* obituary of Collingwood by his son, I had no position and no prospects. Also I had very little of my income left. My cousin, by contrast, in material terms, and in every other way apparently, was prospering very nicely.

I had written an essay printed in *The Criterion* describing the influence of Ruskin on Marcel Proust, and also two essays that had not been accepted for publication on Ruskin as *décadent* and Ruskin as novelist *manqué*. The editor rejected these on the grounds of their intellectual slightness and their episodic nature. I was inclined to believe they were really rejected because of their apparent perversity and an un-pleasant atmosphere, vague and yet penetrating, that derived from a nagging sense of failure and the essential melancholy of my life. For months I experienced no well-being, no optimism. A dark cobwebby atmosphere seemed to envelop and penetrate everything I wrote.

After our intellectual partnership had ended (and how quickly my cousin lost interest in the once joint enterprise!), after the abject failure of my second visit to Coniston, I made no progress with the interviews. I started and abandoned various new approaches. I entertained increasingly unreal, indeed quite ludicrous notions such as acquiring a unique insight into my subject with the aid of spiritualists. Since I could see no possibility of persuading the châtelaine, the person best qualified to help me, I was foolish enough to enlist the help of a latter-day Sludge, who relieved one gullible young man of some of his small inheritance without achieving any worthwhile results.

A sort of breakdown marked my definite abandonment of the project. In hospital, a small sanatorium, a Nerve sanatorium, I dreamed regularly of Coniston. I saw face to face the man on the rain-soaked steamer jetty — not an anonymous prowler but the image of Ruskin familiar to me from the photographs of his old age. Usually in such dreams the man would slowly turn to face me, the pathetic eyes beneath the shaggy eyebrows would plead with me not to question him. I interpreted this as signifying that I was looking for confirmation that I was right to abandon what had become a sickly sort of obsession.

On one occasion, however, in a variation of one of these recurring dreams, the old man spoke to me; he told me that the tardy removal of restrictions on his experiencing physical love, the realization too late in life that 'a living wife is better than a Dead World' had made his final years years sometimes poisoned by regret, sometimes a constricting nightmare. He had feared death greatly, he said, but was not sure that death was not preferable to the prospect of disgracing himself before his friends and the world and setting to nought the exemplary rectitude of a lifetime. For that reason and because of all the usual humiliating mean miseries of age, all the stupors and the anguishes of his enfeebled final decade, he had come to envy the early deaths of lax, disorderly, reprehensible talents like Shelley or Byron, or that German dramatist who had ended his 'fumy, rockety-sputter of a life, brandy-heated' on the threshold of middle age. It was he, not the Severns, who had discouraged visitors; he was the one who had exacted promises for a bonfire of his private correspondence.

The dream was so coherent, so vivid that on waking I wished I could have reassured the old man that our researches had discovered nothing at all to harm his reputation. On the contrary he remained one Great Victorian to have retained his complexity and his 'virtue'. So far no lurid popularizing revelations had emerged to be stamped like a brand of infamy across those unhappy, vulnerable, uncertain features . . .

At the small Nerve sanatorium, in a spa town, I spent a good deal of my time sleeping. Of course there were the sessions spent with the doctors but from my layman's point of view I felt a certain tentativeness, a certain lack of direction and serious commitment to successful therapy in their whole approach. However, this was not true of the brisk little German or central European who gave me the most interesting and varied tests, which included noting my reactions to a series of photographs inserted in an epidiascope and flashed on to a white wall in his partially darkened surgery. When a bearded patriarch appeared on the wall I knew very well that it was not Ruskin. (It looked more like Tolstoy in the dress of a moujik.) Nevertheless something prompted me to say Ruskin at this unexpected apparition. The next image was of a young woman asleep, or perhaps she was dead, perhaps she was lying in state. She had the features of a princess and was elaborately coiffured. A photographer with his stand camera and funereal focusing-cloth was standing next to the bed, in readiness to take her portrait. I muttered facetiously Ilaria di Caretto, which must have strained the analyst's ingenuity to interpret. I was shown several pictures of towers, including the Eiffel Tower, a New York skyscraper and St Mark's bell-tower. After the last I said Rose La Touche. One image caused a powerful reaction in me which of course the doctor noted and no doubt found highly significant. This was the picture of a girl in a summer frock that at first I confused with the friend of Violet Severn. (Not all the pictures were easy to make out since the room was not in total darkness.) The girl in question was sitting in a deck-chair in a garden, a wooden fence beyond. She was shown in profile, looking downwards in a pose that suggested meditation (if not mere embarrass-ment). The profile was pure, austere. The shadow of a bird-house on a pole — the pole also had short arms like a lamppost — lay across greensward, across the girl's floral dress and across the greensward beyond as far as the back

134

fence. I studied the girl and every detail of the slightly out of focus background with an air of intense concentration while the doctor made notes, but I lost interest as soon as I was certain that my first assumption had been mistaken. (How could such a coincidence possibly occur?) The garden was not at Brantwood. The indistinct background beyond the garden did not contain any hills. There was some kind of structure in the distance, an artificial structure that might have been an electricity pylon. The girl was no one I had ever seen. Sensitive-looking, demure, but not cold and withdrawn, she was only a little like the girl I had mistaken her for.

Compared to the pictures flashed on the wall, the word-association tests were extremely boring. My answers as usual were said to be highly significant. The dreams I related were often invented or were memories of Ruskin's dreams. For instance, I retold Ruskin's dream of an Italian journey undertaken alone except for the company of a firefly. On the second day, at twilight, the firefly weaved around him like an electric sparkler, making ever more intense golden letters that spelled out Rose's name before disappearing. In my version I changed the floral name to Violet.

The doctor, even if he had realized what I was doing, would have had an impossible task separating the various strands of truth and fabrication and borrowings. My conscience was untroubled. Ruskin's were surely outstandingly interesting dreams for any analyst to get his teeth into.

To complicate matters still further, some of the dreams I borrowed from Ruskin I emended or even reversed. The dream of Ruskin on St Mark's campanile looking in vain for Rose La Touche where she said she would be standing on the chequered stones of the great piazza, I rearranged as a dream in which I had stood on the campanile looking out over the lagoon, not thinking to wave to the girl down below whose fear of heights had prevented from accompanying me. I added as a note of pathos that the girl in my dream, stung into tears by my callous forgetfulness, had been comforted by a mature, grey-haired Italian gentleman with handlebar moustaches, beautiful manners and a warm heart.

I did not always set out to produce deliberate travesties of Ruskin's dreams. In some cases a simple lapse of memory near the start of my account made it seem more natural to develop the dream in a new direction. As Warwick once said in a cynical mood:

— Imagination equals an imperfect memory.

The magic lantern interlude had taken place in a nearby Victorian villa in its own grounds. The villa had a masque of the red death entrance. Ruby-red diamond panes predominated in the coloured glass of the front porch that was also a miniature conservatory. The surgery with white walls for magic lantern projection contained a huge double-sided desk which stood before windows hung with heavy brown curtains. Despite the width and height of the bay, these curtains had evidently been intended for more palatial casements; they bulged like a dirty fog bank in the Lake District or like the drapes that bulge between pillars in the piazza and the piazzetta in Venice (seeing them reminded me that not many months earlier I had drunk sweetish beer and had eaten a small cake at a table outside the *Quadri*), and on the floor they spread and surged right up to the huge flat-topped desk like the sea encountering a massive boulder. On another wall, a curtainless narrow window overlooked grounds locked in winter frost with some bare, contorted, starveling trees in the distance. Even after the doctor had begun to examine me, I was still describing the house and the room to myself for Warwick's benefit, a habit of long-standing, although I had no intention of writing to him. I had a physical examination first of all. The doctor said I was very small and thin but that I was probably very wiry. He was a short man himself but thickset. He asked me when I had had my tonsils removed. After I denied ever having an operation in my life, although I had been delicate as a child, he grew

136

immediately very heated and made impatient gestures, then he decided to conceal his exasperation in a sudden, all-too-obviously sham assumption of bonhommie as though he was an actor in very broad comedy on the stage. Until he began to speak and gesticulate, I had taken him for an Englishman with a swarthy complexion.

Warwick did not visit me. I received few letters. The circumstances surrounding one letter that I did receive I have never properly explained. An envelope was given to me one day at breakfast-time: a blue envelope with a large smudge on it that reminded me of Mrs Elms's habitual stigmata and of the copy of *Sesame and Lilies* with the dirty thumbprint on its cheap blue binding. The name on the envelope was not mine. I pointed this out at once. The name was practically illegible. It looked a little like 'Fulcher' or 'Vulture'. I joked with the nurse that I was not 'Mr Vulture'. I was persuaded to open it but when I was able to demonstrate that the letter was addressed to someone called John, they were forced to recognize a mistake had been made and I never saw the letter again. Was it an experiment to test my reactions and gauge the extent of my deviation from the normal?

At first my Ruskin obsession continued at full spate despite the strange surroundings and my realization that the obsession was threatening my mental stability. My inner 'fortalices of strength'. To some extent I resented the doctors but I did not quite regard my sessions with them as encounters with 'fiends in daily temptations'. The dream of Ruskin, the genuine dream, the man on the jetty, I have already mentioned.

My thoughts often returned to the Brantwood sale. Why had I restricted my purchases to personal belongings of the great man? And why had I purchased nothing at all on the final day? Any scrap of paper with John Ruskin's signature would have been an item to treasure. The thought that I had missed a chance that was unlikely ever to recur caused me torment.

I was not actively encouraged to read. I had naturally no opportunity to continue serious studies. But light fiction was not forbidden me. For example, I read Agatha Christie's *Murder at the Vicarage*. Later, by accident, I borrowed *The Old Curiosity Shop* from another patient and, although I do not remember this at all clearly, I was told I threw the book on the floor in a brief tantrum. (Perhaps I shouted: 'All foul fiction is leze majesté to the Madonna and to womanhood', furious with the author for having 'killed' Little Nell for the sake of the market.) My identification with Ruskin, although limited and intermittent, was at times embarrassingly obvious. One day I bawled at some visitors to go away. They had arrived on a rainy day. They wore raincoats and were carrying disgustingly smelly wet gamps. It is hard to say, in this particular case, whether the identification was with Ruskin or with Violet Severn.

I was, as I estimate, in a seriously disturbed condition for between three weeks and a month. It was during those weeks that I complained of headaches brought on by listening to a drummer drumming away on a scratched dance-music record — something no one else could hear; and consequently there were questions about how frequently I had noticed such hallucinations in the past? When had they started? Had I experienced any other kind of hallucination? I told the doctors of a voice speaking to me in a monotone, emphasizing each word by pauses: 'You . . . don't . . . know . . . all . . . the . . . facts.' I did not tell them about the girl and the old man I had seen at Coniston. More and more I came to believe they had not been any ordinary man and girl but it seemed such a complicated, rarefied story to embark on . . .

I remember writing during the first weeks to a friend — not Warwick (by this time I was laying the foundations of a resistance to Warwick's influence and importance in my life) — that everything was very tranquil where I was — dreary and provincial and strange — but certainly the effect was calming. Later I asked this friend if my letters had been altogether rational. He said they were in most respects but at the end of one of them I had written: 'The password is Vichy Water.' And I had signed myself 'J. Rusconi'. My friend would not show me that particular letter. Perhaps he was afraid that the sight of it might undo weeks of rest and therapy.

Perhaps he was right.

After my 'cure' I had been warned that until some new meaningful activity or some strong emotion took the place of my former obsession I would feel dispirited and apathetic and would suffer from a diminished sense of reality.

In the opinion of my relatives, after insanely frittering away my inheritance, I was lucky to obtain even the modest job I did get even if this involved moving to a part of the country to which I had a decided aversion. I know I obtained the position because of my degree. This was a cause of friction between my non-graduate colleagues and myself. And my immediate superior was forever labouring the point that I must keep both feet on the ground to make progress.

The financial aspect aside, I was never able to find any incentive to work. In the end only the structure of an imposed routine enabled me to keep going. I hoped that as I grew older I might be less susceptible to painful if trivial impressions, also that I might lose the overwhelming sense of waste and of enduring an atmosphere so hostile to my physical and mental well-being. I came to regard old age and retirement, though so impossibly far off, as 'the sanctuary swept and garnished' or as one of the great grey areas of emptiness Warwick had spoken of; if it proved to be even narrower than my present confines, at least it should be more relaxed, more equable, without the continual sharp, small stresses that I could rarely distance myself from.

Illogically I imagined this kind of quietist future for myself at the same time that I believed war to be imminent and inescapable and the human race faced with extinction. We would all go together I often thought — dangerous and ineffectual dreamers of all kinds — swept down like the spiders' webs in a potting shed that is going to be thoroughly cleaned out.

Unlike many of my contemporaries, whose commitment to the arts became gradually (or with dramatic suddenness) subordinated to a new political commitment, the spectre of Communism did not beckon to me as Munich approached.

If I had seen much of Warwick at the time I am sure I would have been less comfortable with his semi-serious advocacy of Fascism than his old iconoclasm on the subject of the arts, religion, ancient institutions, clichés and accepted ideas, and the lives of newspaper celebrities and national leaders. The post-war dictators had been clowns to Warwick at first. At Oxford any kind of jingoism had been anathema to him. Even at Coniston I remembered him saying that the greatest claptrap in the whole of Ruskin was the phrase 'the deep hearts of nations'.*

It came as no great surprise the next time we met to learn that Warwick's political allegiances had swung from one extreme to the other. Meanwhile I remained in much the same old non-political rut — or, if to be non-political is as impossible as we are so often told, the same old unconsciously-political rut — too self-centred to concern myself continuously with the world's clearly desperate predicament. As far as my private life was concerned almost everything happened as Warwick had facetiously foretold. I became more and more the timid, habit-constrained, anxiety-ridden, finer-grained solitary of a Henry James story in an environment from which the only kind of air, the special air that I needed, had been removed by a special kind of air-pump. Much less forceful than the obsessed John Marcher. More like Morris Gedge during his purgatorial years as librarian at Blackport-on-Dwindle. Like Herbert Dodd on his bench of desolation.

---

*Conclusion to Hesperid Aeglé chapter *Modern Painters* V. Apart from this 'blemish', one of the most ornately beautiful passages in Ruskin.

The backwater which Warwick had foretold for me turned out to be life in an Insurance office and, out of office hours, life in a new avenue of substantial, colourless (pebble-dash), withdrawn and private houses, with dark cold high narrow rooms to complement their respectable, forbidding exteriors — houses that a detached observer might well think admirably suited rigid, unlikeable people living alone. The modern settlement petered out in a few acres of grazing land, a tiny reservoir, and a view of two recently finished cooling towers. The brave future that the houses and the towers seemed to portend and hoped to share was a respectable, tidy, perfectly regulated, sanitized modern age of the utmost rectitude and decorum, a purer Victorian age with Belisha beacons, no traffic accidents, no violent crime. In fact only the faintest, most unobtrusive signs of life were noticeable in the avenue, such as the hand belonging to an elderly female across the way that tentatively, stealthily, moved a wash leather in tiny circles on the clear glass of an upstairs window between and above lace curtains.

I hated the house. I hated the books on the wall, the dead things Ruskin had spoken of, that I kept high up in a blue-grey cupboard with glass doors. A pallid and joyless light fell on my books from a rear window that overlooked not a garden or backyard but a whitewashed outhouse with a sloping glass roof, that contained the latest in washing machines and some geraniums in pots along a broad shelf. On desolate wet evenings the rain patterd dismally and discreetly on the glass roof.

Warwick and I met one last time. The circumstances exceptional but prosaic — family business.

Warwick had been married three or four years. The wedding had taken place shortly after I left the Nerve Sanatorium. An invitation had been sent to me but I hadn't attended the ceremony.

Warwick's wife was expecting a baby. Their second child.

141

After the afternoon's business, we spent the evening together at a concert. Then we caught late trains to our respective towns — Warwick back south, my own train west to Liverpool Lime Street.

The concert programme was the kind you expect in a large provincial town which the Hallé or another orchestra visits a few times a year. Inevitably the programme will include Beethoven's Fifth or his *Pastoral*, Dvorak's *New World*, or Tchaikovsky's Fifth or *Pathétique*. That evening it was Beethoven's *Pastoral*.

The handsome concert hall in green and cream (Venetian gothic windows on the façade facing the market hall) had a balcony on three sides, a large organ behind the players. On Sundays the hall was a Methodist church.

Our seats were downstairs next to a yellow pillar. To the left of us a ground glass window darkened as the evening wore on. In quiet passages, as well as hearing the same mortified, ladylike cough, I was aware of a downpour outside, rain clattering on the flags of an invisible yard or a back alley beyond this window.

Warwick raised the forbidden topic of Ruskin. Did I recall what Ruskin had said about the composer we were about to hear?

Beethoven? I thought for a moment.

— Beethoven: a toolbag dropped on the floor.

Warwick remembered in more detail that Ruskin had said the composer sounded to him like the upsetting of bags of nails 'with here and there an also dropped hammer'.

During the interval Warwick asked if I intended staying in the line I was in.

— I don't think I have much choice, I told him. Except to move a little further down the same rut.

— You could have been a teacher, Warwick said. A librarian?

Broaching the forbidden subject again, he asked if I had changed my mind about Violet Severn.

— Why do you say that? I asked.

— Oh, I don't know, he said. Sometimes I think she wasn't quite the woman we took her to be. I think we tended to see no further than her shyness. After all, you were dreadfully shy as a child. Whenever there were visitors at Brantwood, that Coniston woman told us, Violet always found something that needed her attention in her room. When grown-ups called I remember you used to disappear. But there was slightly more to you than simple bashfulness.

Warwick added:

— Do you remember her telling us about the hours Violet spent fussing with her hair? Violet, who never had any interest in the male sex! Violet, the wiry, independent outdoor-woman!

— We don't know that she had no interest in men, I said.

— Quite, said Warwick.

While I listened to the music I pictured Violet Severn gazing at herself in despair in a bedroom mirror, her lank hair lanker and much greasier than when she had first started to brush it, her eyes sore, her eyebrows painful and rigid from long fixed staring . . . Ruskin had said that the one genuine interest a suburban unmarried woman always had was in new hairstyles and the latest fashions that originated with Parisian prostitutes 'of the lowest order' . . . A dressing-table with hinged side-mirrors that had belonged to Violet's mother had been among the miscellaneous household effects auctioned in the garden at Brantwood. I imagined Violet as a young girl (Mrs Rigby had a photograph of Violet aged twelve or thirteen) adjusting the angles of those mirrors to obtain fresh perspectives on her features.*

After the concert Warwick and I talked briefly of old times. Friends and teachers at Oxford. The loquacious

---

*Like Violet Severn, in adolescence I was obsessed by my appearance. I used to hold up a hand mirror at right angles to a mirror on the wall in order to study my beak of a nose. My uncle, Warwick's father, once said that my nose had continued to grow long after the rest of my face.

elderly female relative who, whenever you told her anything, immediately found a parallel in her own experience. (If the parallel was obvious, she would start her account of it by 'Like . . .', if the connection was at all tenuous, with great energy, resourcefulness and relish, she would begin 'Not like . . .'. In this way she was able to convert every word uttered to her into interminable reminiscences of her younger days).

Warwick wanted to know if I remembered the 'Dowager' who used to say:

— My grandfather was a Peregrine, you know.

— No one could have looked more like one, I joined in.

— Have you still got all that Ruskin material? Warwick asked.

I said I had.

He shook his head.

I asked him did he still drink to forget the next war.

He said I should have gone to fight in Spain. It would have given me a new perspective on my life in Liverpool.

Obviously Warwick was quite prosperous. He had a car but he said he rather dreaded it breaking down and preferred the train for long journeys.

I would not have known where to start to describe honestly and comprehensively my own life, even had I thought Warwick would have had the patience to listen. Once it had been axiomatic with me that you could not be deprived of a love of aesthetic experiences whatever your external circumstances. I had not reckoned on entirely losing my appetite for such things.

After spending so many years believing myself to be nurturing my aesthetic sense, convinced that it was the most profound, inviolable, permanent part of my nature, I had begun to doubt its value, its existence even. Those cocksure theorists who denied the existence of the aesthetic sense as 'a distinct kind of mental activity' were probably right. I regretted now that I had not had the satisfaction of bringing my study of Ruskin to a successful conclusion. I believed I might have done if I could have seen it narrowly as a means of personal advancement. I could have fudged and faked and papered over cracks and, once it had served its purpose, put the revered (respectable) bust back on the shelf.

On the way to the station we negotiated large puddles created by the recent downpour. A picture palace's electric sign, the colour of blue chalk, was reflected in a canal. Warwick claimed that a fur-coated woman, hatless and with permanent waves in her black hair, standing beneath a streetlamp, was an ageing woman of the streets. Almost superannuated. He referred to her as Pharaoh's Oldest Daughter, Fatima with the Splendid Wig . . . Since that day I have not set eyes on my cousin. Each year I receive a Christmas card — a reminder of the names of the children, any change of address — in a female hand.

Just after the war I made a brief visit to Coniston on a half-day motor-coach excursion. I was staying at Ambleside in a boarding-house still lit by gas. In the second half of the 1940s that already seemed very antiquated. On the train to Windermere I shared a corridorless compartment with two bovine young women, very stout and inappropriately dressed for the lakes and mountains, one in a mauve, one in an olive-green tailored suit; the women reeked of perfume and they wore demi-veils with their hats, a fashion that had not lost for me associations with much earlier days; those veils and the yellowing photographs of lakes and fells between the backs of the seats and the luggage nets made the railway journey seem a little like a journey into the past.

I set out for Coniston one rainy afternoon. I had seen the trip advertised outside a newsagents. The coach was less than half full. By then Coniston Water was most commonly associated with Malcolm Campbell and record water speed attempts. However, despite the presence of mechanics and dinghies (I had looked into a boathouse for a glimpse of *Bluebird*, but only saw tarpaulin-covered small boats) and despite the groups of sight-seers who had come on a wet day only because this was the scene of the record-breaking attempts, for me it remained the same old melancholy Victorian lake dominated by the house on the east bank and filled with memories of the two periods I had spent in the area.

I paid a call on Mrs Rigby. She didn't recognize me straightaway. She was very much altered herself. She had grown very stout and walked about her small cottage by holding on to the furniture. Her voice had altered and she was much less fluent in her conversation. She had lost her mother and her husband.

When I inquired about Violet Severn, I learned that Violet was dead also.

I asked if Miss Severn had been happier once she had moved to the village.

— No more ghosts? I said.

Mrs Rigby hoped that she hadn't exaggerated what Violet had described.

— Poor Violet, Mrs Rigby sighed. She didn't take to life in the village. She felt the streets hemmed her in. She felt stifled. And she had been out of touch with village affairs for so long, she had nothing in common with the people round here.

Mrs Rigby wanted to know about my book. When I said the book had never been completed, she thought that seemed a pity and a waste. It was impossible to tell whether she was genuinely disappointed.

I told her that for the last ten years I had worked in an Insurance office in Liverpool. As I spoke I could hardly bear to think of the ox-blood walls of the building in Dale Street, the Kardomah café where I had my midday meal, the station where I caught the electric train each evening to suburban Waterloo . . .

I had not been in the war. My poor eyesight . . .

She was curious about the bombing in Liverpool . . .

146

My personal history? . . .

As Warwick had always predicted I had not marrried . . .

Mrs Rigby twice referred to Warwick as my brother, the same mistake Violet Severn had made. I said there was little I could tell her about him. He had seen a good deal of action in the war. He had a family. Three girls. We exchanged Christmas cards.

A little later she asked after him again. What did I say his rank had been in the army? She apologized for her failing memory.

She wanted me to scatter breadcrumbs from the kitchen table on the back path for the birds. She had not done this earlier because her cat had been outside. I asked about the cats, Mazzie and Snip. Mrs Rigby seemed surprised and touched that I remembered their names. Mazzie had lived to be nearly fourteen. Her present cat was a young brindled tom cat, Captain, named after the cat in *Mrs Dale's Diary*.

Foxgloves at the end of the garden were slender skeletal structures with just a nosegay of purple or white flowers left at the top. Foxglove petals were scattered on the soil. A profusion of yellow loosestrife had also shed petals. The recent rain had brought all the scents out of the wild flowers, the rank grass, the nettles and ferns. Bees hovered. Gnats juggled. After dutifully throwing breadcrumbs down on the drying path, I went back indoors. Moments later the garden was black with birds.

Mrs Rigby's library book lay on the rep tablecloth, with a large fringed bookmark sticking out at both ends: the book was a ghost story or mystery called *The Shadow of the Newel Post*. Like its predecessor, the present cat lay curled up on the tablecloth.

— I don't believe there is much interest in Ruskin nowadays, Mrs Rigby remarked. At any rate, not around here. It's all speed records on the lake now.

I asked her if she had seen much of Violet Severn after she moved to the village.

— Not a great deal, she said.

I interpreted the look she gave me as meaning: Why should you be interested now that you have abandoned your book?

Daniel Rigby had died suddenly. Before the war. Her mother had outlived him by more than six years. A good thing her husband couldn't see the wilderness the back garden had become. It was too much for an old woman with rheumatism.

With the disconcerting candour of the old, she told me I looked almost a different person I was so changed.

— You and your brother were such nice serious young students, she added.

The motor coach was parked in the village. I doubt if any of the excursionists from Ambleside had taken a look at Brantwood that afternoon. I hadn't been there myself. Mrs Rigby said the house had been used as a school in the war. After leaving her cottage I spent a few minutes in the church. Another few minutes I reserved for the little Ruskin museum. I was the only visitor there to look at the Rock Harmonicon, the spines of his books in English and translation, the 'noble dog' portrait by Arthur Severn. I walked quickly past the end of the street where my lodgings had been. Although it seemed most unlikely that Mrs Elms would still be alive, the unpleasant associations were enough to make me hurry past. That street, like the rest of Coniston was little changed I thought, but then my visit was very brief.

It was drizzling again when I returned to the bus. The bus set off earlier than scheduled as soon as all the passengers were back on board. People complained about the weather. No one gave the impression of having enjoyed the half day.

— A dead and alive sort of place, a woman behind me declared.

Her friend agreed it had been a disappointment.

Most of the passangers seemed as undecided about Coniston on their departure as on their arrival.

The traffic on the roads was light. A last glimpse of the delicate dusk on the lake might have suggested a scene in a Maeterlinck play. The sight of the famous speedboat at full throttle would certainly have destroyed the dreamy symbolist associations of its name. A few schoolboys at the rear of the coach gazed back with the forlorn hope of seeing *Bluebird* on the dim water.

Soon after this brief visit, on a blank page in the last of a number of exercise books (just below the final paragraph of my abandoned biography), I wrote: Ruskin dead (1900) Joan Severn dead (1924) Arthur Severn dead (1931) W.G. Collingwood dead (1932) Violet Severn dead (1941?).

Nowadays I no longer have any genuine interest in John Ruskin or in literature in general. Whenever I pass a bookshop window, such as the one near the office in Dale Street, I recognize of course the sort of book I used to read. Among the latest publications by new authors I recognize the books that I think I might have been attracted to if I still read. However I am not interested enough to go inside and examine them. Not even a biography of Ruskin I saw in the window the other day. By Derrick Leon. I may have misspelt the name.

I hate darkness, I believe, as much as Ruskin did. Like Ruskin I am at the farthest remove from the prowler drawn to lamplight and shadows, poverty and vice. The type of man, for example that Dickens was. For Ruskin, Dickens was leader of 'the steam-whistle party *par excellence*', only concerned with effects that would be understood by the pit. 'Steam' (and 'Rockety' and 'Fumy' to a lesser extent) were epithets Ruskin applied incontinently with the blunted force of over-used expletives. 'Steam' was his favourite. Infinitely protean, it became detached from its original specific

149

meaning in the strange and varied contexts to which he introduced it.

The artistic Imperator watched 'costumes' not 'women' from his window. The Slade Aristarchus from time to time descended to the railway carriage, made occasional forays into the world of the Pentonville omnibus. Denunciation his forte. A preacher rabid to bite other preachers. The moral fanatic rebuked the artist in himself. The world of art critic was an assize court in perpetual session. But finally the 'prodigal voice grew dumb'. Deprived of his faculties, his strength gone, his razor-sharp weapons removed, he sat, a coy pelican, a lion with leaf claws. Perhaps there were memories from time to time. When he closed his eyes the sound of a cup rattling in its saucer perhaps echoed in a greater silence, in the vaster emptiness of a Palazzo or Grand Hotel formerly a palace. Perhaps there were visions of mountains and cathedrals. A view of 'the yet undestroyed ramparts'. Some fragments of 'time-worn wall, and dark arcade'. The end of Venice in a fading Giorgione fresco. Masts outlined in fire against San Giorgio Maggiore. Boats moored off the Zattere. 'Such a morning as this on the white Salute is enough to raise one from the gates of death.'

It grieves me to realize that it was my cousin's and my own cruel importunings that gave Miss Severn nightmares of her childhood long after she thought she had escaped from the darkness. Of course the real septuagenarian was not the bogeyman Violet saw him as but as a child she was understandably afraid of his infirm silences, his infirm despair, his terrible infirm despairing rages.

It grieves me too that we failed to recognize Violet's distinction, for too long resting complacently in our mistaken first assumption that she was insensitive, unappreciative, uncultured, a farouche barbarian. Perhaps we can be forgiven. Violet deceived everyone. She deceived shrewd old

Collingwood. Where most of the others were flatterers, confidence men, *arrivistes*, derivationists, epigones, Violet, I believe, was an original; her greater genuineness accounted for the deep contempt she felt for the disciples and pilgrims and lion-hunters, perfect in their observance of the correct forms, but vain and hypocritical and unaware of the reptilian triteness of all their spoken and written utterances.

The young girl and the old man, who were they? I have said that Warwick took a snapshot of the girl. That this came into my possession when Warwick lost all interest in our project and that the print was disfigured by faint halations he couldn't account for. These halations have grown more noticeable with time. Now that I study them closely, they are like flames playing about the girl's breasts and loins, and although there is nothing obviously immodest in the girl's pose, there seems something sensual and perverse about her that I never noticed before — this girl of the same physical type as Rose La Touche, *la bella Simonetta*, a Princess of Este by Pisanello, Carpaccio's St Ursula, Ilaria di Caretto — the pallor of love and death on her brow, a cold melancholy in her eyes.

Was the prowler also the apparition breathing upon the glass?

Surely the apparition was a figment born of the fear the American scholar and my cousin and I had revived, that had lain dormant for so many years? Violet had responded with sympathy to the American woman's researches until she saw into what infernal regions she was being drawn back. Hadn't she set her face against us out of fear of reviving those 'deaf blind speechless unspeakable rages', the memory of those eyes that, in life, already appeared 'sealed by the earth darkness'?

Is it conceivable that Violet Severn could have created and exteriorized those phantoms, the old man and the girl, out of

151

the extremity of her own fear and obsession, her own dark visions — like images thrown on to a screen that others (certain others) could also see?

The only photograph of Violet I have ever seen shows her as a twelve-year-old with a disdainful look. No likeness to the unprepossessing middle-aged spinster she was to become. A proud, austere face. Almost beautiful. The features not unlike those of the girl Warwick and I had seen with Violet and the old man.

The more I study Warwick's 'spirit photograph', the more obvious the resemblance becomes between the nameless girl and the picture of the young Violet shown to us by Caroline Rigby. At the time neither Warwick nor I had paid much attention to Violet's portrait.

I have too many theories. There is too little firm ground.

I have never seriously believed in the supernatural.

I am sure he never intended to frighten the daughter of the much-loved cousin who nursed him in his old age — Joan's youngest child and favourite. His delight in young girls in their springtime had been a constant factor in his life. Surely he was incapable of meaning Violet any harm. His vacant smiles at her through the window no doubt were intended to convey benevolence, kindness, graciousness.

Who won the battle? Apollo's battle with Hesperid dragon or python? 'The strife of purity with pollution . . . of life with forgetfulness . . . of love with the grave.'